BooK

1

The Amazing Adventures of Captain Thomas Mc Leary and his faithful friend, his Germany Sheppard dog, Mc Leary.

Thomas' adventure begins when he decided to save a young girl's life by doing a walk of life from Glasgow to Penzance to raise funds. With Jodie Mc Fadden who writes for the newspaper and tells his exploits, the first 1 S.A.S. was formed during the 2 World War, known as The Originals.

To Hugh and Chris
all the best.

[signature]

BOTTLES OF COURAGE

Stephen W Rouse

authorHOUSE®

AuthorHouse™ UK
1663 Liberty Drive
Bloomington, IN 47403 USA
www.authorhouse.co.uk
Phone: UK TFN: 0800 0148641 (Toll Free inside the UK)
        UK Local: (02) 0369 56322 (+44 20 3695 6322 from outside the UK)

Published by AuthorHouse   01/12/2024

ISBN: 979-8-8230-8602-8 (sc)
ISBN: 979-8-8230-8603-5 (e)

Library of Congress Control Number: 2024900410

Print information available on the last page.

Any people depicted in stock imagery provided by Getty Images are models,
and such images are being used for illustrative purposes only.
Certain stock imagery © Getty Images.

This book is printed on acid-free paper.

CONTENTS

CHAPTER 1

NO MAN'S LAND

Centered, among an encampment of army tents in the desert of North Africa, we home in on Captain Black, an officer mid-thirties bearded with a sort of tan, desert uniform, a field revolver by his side and an eye patch from an old wound, wearing S.A.S Beret. It's the first branch of S.A.S come to be known as "The Original".

He is alone and nothing stirs quietness around the camp. Only the moon, like a silver plate, lights the silhouettes of the tents against the deserted landscape of the never-ending wilderness. Wearily, he looks at his watch, "23.00" he mutters to himself as he re-enters his own tent, where a single swinging lamp is the only source, of illumination. The Captain's tent is bare, a single wooden bed and chair, table, half empty bottle old Malt Whisky with a metal cup next to the bottle.

He draws up his chair, sits and looks mournfully at four dog tags. These soldiers, he knows, will never return. Then he picks up one dog tag that reads Lt Mc McFadden.

Looking down, a moment passes, he takes a breath, smiles, reaches for his fountain pen, that his wife and daughter gave him at Paddington Station before this mission, gazes at their photo which lies next to a pad of S.A.S letters headed: S.A.S DIVISION N.A. NUM 1.

He gazes at his watch as he starts to write, pour a wee (little) dram of Whisky. Take a quick nip.

"Time, now 23.00.45:

Sergeant Thomas McLeary returned to camp having gone AWOL behind enemy lines for two weeks.

With him he brought his C/O, Lt Mc McFadden, who had also been missing for just over two weeks on a mission attempting to discover potential enemy strategies.

With him he brought a wounded German officer who was in possession of plans which shed light on the future movement of the upper echelons like the Desert Fox Rommel of the German High Command. These plans have been dispatched to HQ. Their importance cannot be underestimated.

Therefore, I recommend that both Thomas McLeary and Lt McFadden be awarded the highest commendations. I would also like to recommend that Sgt McLeary is given a commission. Just a footnote, Sir, and with respect, can you please add, if possible, that the Sergeant's dog, McLeary also be awarded a medal for bravery.

Sincerely, Captain Black S.A.S DIV 1/1942 North Africa. Christmas day"

12 HOURS EARLIER

War, desert terrain seen through the haze of a battle. Mortars light up the sky like a firework display. Small arms fire echo in the background and tracer bullets penetrate the night sky. As the sounds of war recede so the haze lifts, the morning sun starts to slowly rise over the sand dunes like giant ant hills.

Sergeant Thomas McLeary slowly opens his eyes.

He is aged late 40's, in camouflage desert gear, unshaven and darkly tanned face and arm, with panda eyes from wearing sun goggles to protect them He comes out from hiding, draws back his bedroll open, his military can, washes his face and wipes his eyes. By his side a faithfully friend, a dog, a black shaggy Alsatian called McLeary crawls out.

Thomas pours some water into his Army helmet. Thomas: "I'm going for a piss boy, stand guard."

McLeary doses a soft bark, as he looks up from lapping his water.

Thomas returns. There is a sound of some kind of engine approaching. Thomas dives for cover, takes out his field glasses, as he pears through the light desert haze. He sees a motorbike patrol, puts down his glasses. Suddenly the sun hits a shining object lying in the sand. Thomas grabs his field glass, sees the body of a young officer, Lt McFadden, lying face down in the sand. The Sun light reflecting off his S.A.S. hip flask. Thomas slowly reaches back and maneuver, his rifle into position and attaches the scope

"There is one driver" Thomas mutters to himself, "And a high ranking German Officer, in the sidecar"

Thomas pats McLeary and whispers in his dog's ear. As Thomas's and his dog like a lion going in for the kill move closer to McFadden.

The bike stops a little distance from where McFadden lies. As the driver dismounts, he hands the Officer a Cigarette. Then, as the German soldier, goes to get his lighter out, he sees the British officer who is away a little distance from him. The German soldier reaches for his rifle, and slowly moves forward. Shallow breathing is evidence that "He is still alive", he says to his High Ranking Officer, quietly.

Slowly, deliberately, the muzzle of the German's rifle inches toward the British officer's head. As his finger tightens on the trigger.

Suddenly from out of the shadows, a dog charges and lunges toward the Germans as simultaneously a shot rings out. The German soldier falls to his knees, dead.

As the officer reaches for his gun McLeary leaps on him, take him down. His teeth bite hard into the officer black leather gloved hand. Thomas is there in a single breath. With his revolver at the officers head.

Thomas: "Good Boy! Let go"

Thomas now stands either side of McFadden.

"He's breathing he is still alive, just" Thomas mutters.

Thomas kneels down, lifts McFadden's head, splashes some water from his can, onto a rag then wipes the face of McFadden.

Bending down, he speaks with a Scottish accent to his dog stroking his head.

Thomas: "Good lad, McLeary! Good lad! It's a miracle after two weeks we found him and just in time by the look of things".

Picking Lt McFadden up in a fireman's lift, Thomas mounts the bike with Mc Leary in the sidecar next to the British officer. Thomas points his field revolver at the German officer to mount the bike.

Thomas: "Rouse!"

Officer follows Thomas order holding his wounded arm.

As the sands of the desert are thrown out by the spinning wheel of the bike, they head to HQ.

DESERT NORTH AFRICA 1942 S.A.S CAMP

Captain Black, the commanding officer, stands with his hands behind his back. He looks out across the sands with his good eye toward a Red Cross tent. An old war tore Union Jack at half -mast. Two other S.A.S soldiers stand nonchalantly talking, other S.A.S men go about their daily duties. As one of the S.A.S goes to stamp on the stub of his cigarette, there is the loud crack of a motorbike backfiring.

Everyone automatically dives for cover. As the engine dies, so Captain Black swings round to see. Thomas McLeary on board a German motorcycle. In the sidecar sits Lt McFadden and behind him the wounded

German. Lt McFadden has a German Officer's brown leather attaché case attached to his wrist. McLeary, brings up the rear.

Swinging his tail.

Thomas stops next to the Battle Union Jack. He salutes.

Outside the Red Cross tent. A Doctor, in a white coat with blood stains and two nurse's step out of the tent as two S.A.S men take the German away.

Doctor: "We'll take him now Sergeant."

Thomas and the doctor, with one of the nurses, help MC McFadden onto a stretcher from the sidecar.

Captain Black, counting to five under his breath.

"McLeary." The Captain snaps. "You have always been one for the dramatic. You were under orders that under no circumstances were anyone to go into No Man's Land."

Thomas salutes and stands his ground from the Captain's remark. He slowly brings his hip flask and pours some water into a metal cup for his dog. Thomas then shows his hip flask to the Captain where the following words are engraved. **WHO DARE WINS**

Captain Black looks at the words. Thomas just looks as he tries to explain his actions.

Captain Black understands his loyalty to his Commanding Officer.

''But orders are orders" the Captain says to Thomas's remarks. Thomas knows it's out of his hands.

"It will be up to the big boys to determine your fate" the Captain replies.

Captain then looks at Thomas's dog, Mc Leary, pats him on the head: "Cooks got some Bones for you boy"

Thomas salutes Captain Black and McLeary gives a bark. As they make their way to the cookhouse Captain Black has a small smile on his face.

CHAPTER 2

JUST ANOTHER DAY

Thomas's flat GLASGOW 1960'S

Glasgow tenement, it's 4.00. Clock in the morning stands like a Garnett monument. All the curtains are drawn except one light is visible. Thomas's living room filled with wartime memorabilia.

The mantal piece is an off-white color. On it is Thomas's SAS's hip-flask. Among them, different framed pictures of him on many operations around the world like Indochina, for the British Government.

A breakfast radio show is playing. An old clock, 1960's decor, war medals, pictures of several generations of the McLeary clan in military uniform, and their dogs.

The sound of light snoring reveals Thomas in his seventies, asleep in his old red leather armchair. Beside the chair, on a table, is a framed picture of Thomas McLeary, with his dog and Lieutenant McFadden each wearing their medals. Beneath them, their names are written in ink:

"Thomas McLeary and John McFadden Presented the Victory Cross. Ceremony May 1945. Buckingham Places. Presented by King George"

Early morning street activity. Curtains opening on a New Day. An old woman watches pedestrian passersby from her window. An old man comes out of a doorway. A woman stands with a baby in her arms. They look along the street but we do not see whom they are talking to.

Old woman: "How are you doing Mister McLeary? You've been busy this morning?"

Another woman: "Aye, you'll not catch him in bed for long when he's got messages to do for Thomas".

A group of children among whom we will come to know Hannah, 4 years old, in an old school dress with a light blue ribbon in her hair. Jimmy, he's a little older, dressed in old shorts, a red jumper, stops playing and settles on a stone wall as McLeary passes by.

McLeary is an old shaggy, Alsatian dog with bright eyes and pointed ears. The children all chorus: "What yer got there, McLeary? Anything for us?"

McLeary puts the shopping bag he has been holding in his mouth down on the pavement looks at the children, barks picking the bag up again, heads for a tenement doorway.

The playground is in front of the tenement. Hannah is playing on a swing with her rag doll.

Two local ruffians, Josh and Smokey, both in their late twenties, both wearing, blue jeans, Josh in a black leather jacket, Smokey's in brown, fags in their mouth, have a bone to pick with Ian, Hanna's older brother. They approach the swing and give it a mighty shove so Hannah flies off. Ian, with Jimmy rush over to help her.

Josh, grabbing Ian: "Was it you? Just remember, McKeen, no snitching or you wouldn't see your sixteen's birthday"

Ian: "I have nae"

Smokey: "That was just a warning".

The two ruffians swagger away as Hannah gets unsteadily to her feet.

McLeary stops at the door, drops the shopping bag. Carefully, stands on his hind legs and presses the Buzzer. He waits as the door opens, then picking up the shopping bag, slips inside and carefully makes his way. Up the stairwell.

Two old men outside have just seen what has happened.

"About time the police did something about those two" they remark. Woman: "Aye, but I'd not want to be the ones to cross them".

Hannah is back on the swing with Ian keeping a watchful eye.

The postman cycles up. He has a new red bike. Ringing his silver copper bell stop the bike. Taking a parcel from his bag, spies Ian.

Postman shouts out: "Hi there, young McKeen. Want to earn a wee bar of chocolate?"

Ian nods and runs over to the Postman.

"Take this up to Thomas McLeary. He's been asking for it for a week's".

Giving Ian a small bar of chocolate and the parcel, he cycles off. Ian runs over to Hannah and tells her what he's going to do.

Ian: "Heh, Jimmy, keep an eye on Hannah", Jimmy replies: "no bother. You go on ahead".

McLeary reaches the stairs and trots down the corridor. Reaching a door which is on the latch, he pushes his way in with his nose. The door shuts behind him. McLeary enters the small kitchen, an old cooker in the corner, a table with an old cloth cover it. A couple of wooden chairs but the table is set with white china plates, and knife and fork.

McLeary jumps his Front legs on the table he carefully drops the shopping on top and takes out the bacon goes to the fridge, opens it, places the bacon on a shelf then the eggs close the door and barks.

Thomas is still asleep, snoring. McLeary barks, once more. Thomas wakes, shakes his head and looks at his dog standing in the doorway.

Pushing him-self up slips into his slippers and goes slowly into a hallway that leads to the kitchen. Suddenly there's a knock at the door.

Thomas: "Okay, okay. I can hear you!"

McLeary runs and stands by the door as Thomas reaches the door, pats his dog. Then opens the door. Ian stands there, holding out the parcel.

Thomas: "Ian! Postie too lazy to bring it up himself? Something about an old war wound"

"I Dinnae ken Thomas, but he gave me a bar of chocolate for doing' it". McLeary barks.

Thomas: "Which he didna' tell you, you'd have to share with McLeary here?" McLeary wags his tail and barks at Ian.

"Nae bother, he's my mate, eh boy?"

Ian bends down and ruffles McLeary's neck.

"Postie said you were pining for this. Must be important?." Thomas: "This, to me, Laddie. About the War".

Ian: "Were you a soldier?"

Thomas: "Aye, Laddie, I wasn't always a milkman! Now away with you. You've got school."

JODIE'S ROOM

Jodie's alarm clock rings. Jodie's hand reaches out from under her patch tartan eiderdown and turns the clock off. She throws back the eiderdown and edges to the side of the bed. As she rubs her eyes, she reaches out to switch the radio on next to her bed.

Jodie has long blond lock with a supple firm body, blue eyes. An attractive, intelligent, young girl her early twenties. A copy typist at the local newspaper: The Echo. Her ambition is to become a Reporter for a National newspaper. Her room is cluttered with clothes and female accessories. She is wearing a tight tee shirt and shorts.

Jodie's mother, Mary McFadden calls: "Are you up yet Jodie? Breakfast's almost ready Jodie"

Jodie: "Don't fuss. Ma. I'm up!"

Jodie dances to her wardrobe and talks to her large soft toy a pink elephant sit on a chair in the corner of the room.

Jodie: "Got to look my best today, Pinkie. First impressions that count."

Jodie looks through the clothes on their hangers. Picking out a white top, tartan jeans then spots her brown leather jacket hanging behind the door.

There is a smell of breakfast that fills the kitchen. A radio is on in the background. Thomas is checking the sausages that are grilling. He turns to McLeary, picking up the parcel, opens it to reveal a book.

Thomas: "Okay, Laddie, they smell great. Now. I've been waiting a while for this".

Activity everywhere around the Tenements. Passers by stopping to chat, the Occasional car, a few children playing hopscotch.

A door opens and Jodie comes out. A neighbor dressed in a dressing gown with curlers in her hair picks up the milk from outside her own door.

"Ach, Jodie, aren't you looking grand, today." The woman remarks.

Jodie: "Can'nae stop to blather the day, Mrs. McLean. Can't be late, the new boss at the newspaper. Must make a good impression, but thanks anyway".

Mrs. McLean: "Ach you young folks. Always in a rush. Mind you take care".

Jodie rushes off down the street. The neighbor takes here milk indoors shaking her head.

Thomas looks at the book in his hand and down at McLeary.

Thomas: "Aye, lad. It'll take me back a few years to old mates and to your grandpa. Brave as a lion and certainly earned his medal. Okay, Laddie. let's just see if the bangers are done yet".

McLeary barks. Thomas puts the book back on the table. The title reads "Jock Lewes: The co-founder of the SAS". The whistle of a kettle starts.

ECHO PRESS OFFICE. COFFEE ROOM

The whistle kettle goes off like a train going into a tunnel. The steam pours as it comes to the boiling. Hanging on the coffee room wall is an award to Jodie, for copy typists, of this year. Jodie is making cups of tea and coffee on a tray. A co-worker, Sam, comes in. Sam is tall, busty. Wearing a light top showing a healthy amount of cleavage and jeans. A pack of cigarettes in her breast pocket. Jodie spies.

Sam: "Morning. Looks like we're both trying to impress someone." Jodie grins, as she spoons sugar into the cups.

Jodie: "I've heard he's quite a looker?"

Sam moves over and picks up her tea. Jodie plucks Sam's cigarettes from her pocket, takes out two. Jodie put one in Sam's mouth and one in her own and lights them both.

Jodie: "I've heard he's wee bit old, if ye ken".

Sam: (grins) "Ach well. There something about and good tune played they know how to?

Jodie (wags a large Chocolate finger): "That's no way for a young girl like you to be talking, my girl."

Sam: "And it's not crossed your mind either, by the look of it"

Jodie: "No, I'm hoping he'll want fresh ideas. Give me a real reporting gig. That's my ambition."

Sam: "I don't know about that, but we'd better get back to work otherwise your ambition will be out the window and we'll both be on the brew".

Jodie: "You're right. Give us a hand?"

They finish their cigarettes. Sam exits. Jodie picks up the tray and turns around hurriedly and thinking that Sam will be holding the door, for her. But slams into Stephen, unbeknownst to Jodie, the new editor who walks in. Tea and coffee flying everywhere. Stephen is tall and has an imperious air about him. His pink shirt, blue tie, suit trousers and jacket (dark blue) are soaked. Stephen roars in pain from the scalding hot tea and fury at the state of his clothes. He stands and stares at Jodie in disbelief.

Stephen: "What the hell? Have you no got eyes woman!"

Jodie (indignant): "You no got eyes yoursel'. Wasn't me who tried to break the door down."

Jodie grabs a tea towel from the table and desperately wipes at Stephen tailor made suite and shiny black shoes

Stephen: "I think we need a new tea lady."

Jodie stops and looks up at Stephen who takes the tea towel from her.

Jodie: "I'm Jodie McFadden and I'm not the tea lady. Thank you very much", reply Jodie "I am one of the copy-typists."

Stephen: "Oh, so you're Jodie McFadden. They told me about you at head office". Jodie smiles.

Jodie: "And who are you to be asking questions? Are you part of the new editor's team?"

Stephen: "No, my name's Stephen. But, I'm told the new guys got a short fuse". Jodie: (smiling):

"A short fuse is it? There are a few firecrackers in this office for himself"

Stephen smiles: "He's put a few fires out in his time but, I've just a little tip for you.

Keep your eyes open in future. Bye"

Stephen exits. And Jodie tidy the mess. She looks, a little puzzled after he leaves. Jodie (to herself): "I'll give him keep your eyes open."

Thomas's FLAT - LOUNGE.

There's a noise outside. McLeary pricks up his ears and looks expectantly at Thomas.

They have just finished the eggs and Bangers.

Thomas: "Aye, lad? We know who that'll be, don't we? Friends of yours, let's see what we can find."

As McLeary gets up, Thomas goes off toward the kitchen.

EDITOR'S OFFICE

Jodie enters and sits at her desk next to Sam who is typing. Jodie's clothes are wet.

The other girls are working in the office at various tasks. Sam notices Jodie's wet clothes.

Sam: "Get caught in a storm?"

Jodie (acid): "Oh no! Nothing for you to worry about?"

Just poured coffee and tea over one of the new boys. Actually, you missed your chance; he was tall, dashy and his name's Stephen".

Sam: "I'll keep my eyes open. He's probably one of the new reporters."

Jodie: "It's no' fair. They never think to give people who know the place a chance. They don't think anybody's got brains north of the Watford Gap, or if you don't speak with plum in your mouth, you've no more intelligence than orangutan?"

The office has gone quiet as Stephen walks quietly over to behind Jodie's desk. Jodie is unaware of his presence. Stephen coughs loudly as Jodie jumps out of her skin.

Stephen: "Jodie McFadden, I hope you're better at typing than throwing cups of tea around."

Jodie, Look up, try to grin: "Oh. It's you. I didn't expect anyone to come crashing in doing the Highland fling."

Stephen laughs: "You should see my sword dance. I've to tell you the new editor wants to see you in ten minutes."

Jodie: "Oh no! You didn't tell him about the accident, did you? It wasn't all my fault.

You're not from South of the Watford Gap, are you?"

Stephen: "No and I wasn't born with a plum in my mouth neither. Listen, just be a nice wee girlie as they say here and go see him, okay?"

Jodie looks worried. Sam smiles and gives her the thumbs up as Stephen exits.

CHAPTER 3

HANNA

Thomas's flat GLASGOW 1960'S

Girls and boys stand there, expectantly. All are wearing "hand me downs" and could do with a good scrub. Hannah, the youngest girl in the group has a couple of nasty bruises which look quite ugly from her fall off the swing. Thomas is handing out cartons of milk to each of them. McLeary is in the middle as they all make a fuss of him.

Thomas: "Okay. Nae bother. There's enough for all of you. Jimmy, my boy, how's your Da'?"

Jimmy looks up and hands Thomas his empty carton. Jimmy: "Yam says he's on the mend"

Thomas: "Well, that's grand? Hannah, did we have a wee fall this morning? You'd better get Mum to take you to Doctor Jamieson to have a look at those bruises?"

Hannah: "I'll be fine Mr McLeary, nae bother. They'll go" Thomas: "That's good, if you're all finished?"

Hannah says: "Thomas, can Mister McLeary come out and play?"

Thomas looks down and smiles at her and the rest of the children and then at McLeary.

Thomas: "Up to him, lassie. Shall we ask him?" The children all speak at once.

Children: "Yes...please. yes"

Thomas bends down and cups McLeary's head in his hands and looks him in the eye.

McLeary looks back Thomas.

Thomas: "You want to go play McLeary?" McLeary barks: "OK, then now be off with you mind you be good".

McLeary barks again as they all race off down the stairs and away. Thomas picks up a couple of dropped milk cartons and looks over the balcony to see the children and McLeary running out of the tenement below.

The children and McLeary are playing. McLeary is barking and running around interfering with the boys' football game and trying to catch the Red and Black ball. Hannah is sitting playing with her ragdoll.

McLeary comes over to Hannah and rests his head on her lap. Hannah likes McLeary! Hannah: "You're a good boy"

Jimmy comes over next to Hanna: "We all like him" Jimmy says: "We are bested friends in the whole world"

Jimmy: "Heh, Hannah. You coming? We're going to play by the stream". Hannah looks up and smiles at Jimmy.

Hannah: "Okay, but only if McLeary comes too". Jimmy: "He'll come, nae bother, eh, McLeary.

McLeary barks as the children head off towards the stream. McLeary stops for a second and looks back over his shoulder at Thomas's window. Thomas draws back the curtains of his window and calls down to the kid as they leave the playground:

"McLeary you look after them boy?" McLeary barks.

THE ECHO. EDITORS OFFICE.

Jodie is standing outside the Editor's door. She's got the same feeling as she did when she waited outside the headmaster's door. Nervously she takes the last puff on her cigarette and puts it out. Taking a deep breath, she knocks on the door.

A voice of a man answers "Come in?"

JODIE'S FLAT

Jodie puts the key in the door and opens it. Jodie enters the flat hallway. It is bright, bedecked with family pictures, one of which is of Jodie at school receiving a "Young reporter of the year" award from the mayor. The sound of a Television is on. Jodie's mother, Alice, is in the kitchen preparing dinner. Jodie stops at the picture, takes it off the wall and studies it. She shrugs sadly. Alice comes out of the kitchen into the hallway

Alice: "What's up with you, my girl? You look as if you've lost a pound a found a penny?"

Jodie; "That just about sums up my day but he doesn't seem too bad. His bark's certainly worse than his bite? I'll say that even with a plum in his mouth, and at least I've still got a job."

Alice: "Whose mouths got a plum in it and what's that about a job?" Jodie looks at Alice.

Jodie: "The new boss".

Alice: "Well. I'm sure you made a good impression?"

Jodie: "Impression. You can say that again, Mum. I covered him from head to foot with tea and coffee".

Alice: "Oh, Jodie, you never did. How?"

Jodie: "It wasn't deliberate. How was I to know he was going to open the door."

Alice: "Aye. Well. Never mind… Tomorrow's another day. Come away now, I've made your favorite for dinner, haggis, and neeps. You go and get cleaned up and I'll lay it out".

Jodie replaces the picture. As she goes up to change, Alice reaches through the banisters, takes her hand and smiles.

Alice: "you know, we're both very proud of our wee girl!" Jodie smiles weakly and goes to her room.

Thomas FLAT EVENING

Couching Thomas sitting in his red leather which has seen better days. A cup of tea and biscuits are on the table. He is reading his new book. He puts down the book, looks at the clock, whips his glasses, the clock chimes 7: 00 pm. He's drowsing. He takes a sip of tea.

Thomas yes to himself: "Jock Steel Lewes. His middle name summed him up McLeary! I know there were plenty others brave enough too: Captain Stirling and that madcap, Paddy Blair Mayne but Jock just had that something special. Terrible shame he died so young he never saw life another Christmas nor a woman to love"

Thomas leaves the book open to a picture of a desert camp with Land Rovers in front with Machines Gun on the back ready for action. He gazes, his eyes on the photo of Jock Lewes. They slowly start to close.

NORTH AFRICAN DESERT:

Thomas in a dream sequence with desert, wind, vehicle engines roaring as they traverse the desert, Messerschmitt in flight, guns blazing spitting out empty shell casing. The Desert. Various Jeeps of the Long-Range Desert Group in there pink vehicles. Messerschmitt 109 Fighter planes.

Desert with the convoy of LRDG vehicles, pictures of M110's approaching, guns blazing. One of the vehicles is hit. L.R.D.G vehicle shot up.

There is a loud backfire of a car as Thomas wakes up and closes the book, back in Thomas Flat.

THE STREAM - EVENING

The children are playing by the stream. Charlie sees Hannah's rag doll and grabs it out of her hand. The children chuck it from one to another, keeping it away from Hannah, who desperately tries to intercept and retrieve it. Hannah gives up, walks off ways, sits down and cries. The children continue throwing the rag doll amongst them. McLeary trots over to Hannah and puts his head in her lap. Hannah tries to smile. A shout from Jimmy, cry out and, McLeary, startled, looks toward the stream.

The rag doll is in the water, floating away, there is a light current Hannah cries even louder. As she sees here rag doll slowly flow downstream. The children begin to make their way home. Hannah takes one last look at her disappearing doll and follows them still crying. As McLeary watches her go he turns and runs towards the stream.

3.30 a.m : The orange light from the street lamp lights the room through the curtains. A radiator, Hannah's rag doll is drying. The room is still. A brown chest draws with a mirror is in the corner, a large brass bed with dark blue quilt covering the bed. An old deck chair sit upright with Thomas clothes draped over next to his tartan dressing goon. Thomas's alarm goes off. McLeary pricks up his ears and jumps onto the bed as Thomas sits up. He swings round over the side of the bed and puts on his slippers on rub his hand together.

Thomas: "It's going to be a cold one today, my lad"

Thomas pats McLeary on the head and goes along the hallway into the kitchen.

Starts to get breakfast ready.

THE MRS MCKEEN'S FLAT TENEMENT - EARLY MORNING

Mary McKeen, Hannah's mother is on the phone.

Mary: "Please hurry doctor - she's got a high temperature and bruises on her head and arms. With her father in hospital as well, I'm at the end of my tether".

A few people are already coming and going. It is 4.30 am. Thomas leaves the building with McLeary and walks towards the dairy in the distance. McLeary carries Hannah's rag doll in his mouth. As they reach halfway, an ambulance passes them with lights flashing. Thomas watches as it turns into his tenement street. Stop for a moment.

Hanna's BEDROOM.

Hannah is lying on the bed, very pale. Beside the bed doctor, Jamieson wears a stethoscope, examining her bruises. He takes her pulse. Hannah's mother Mary McKeen watches anxiously. There is a noise outside the room and the ambulance crew enters carrying a stretcher. Mary stands back as the crew set the stretcher out beside the bed.

Jamieson: "Easy does it, now lads."

The crew gently lift Hannah on to the stretcher as the doctor makes some notes. The doctor hands one of the ambulance men the note as the crew begins to wheel Hannah out.

Doctor: "Would you hand this to Doctor Love at the Royal for me? He'll need to see it."

Girl."

Ambulance man: "Aye, sure I will. Right, let's get this poor wee mite to hospital, eh? Noise outside

Mary: "She'll be alright Doctor, won't she?"

Doctor: "I'm sure she will. She's in good hands now. Don't fret yourself. Climb aboard".

CHAPTER 4

THE MILK ROUND

THE MILK DEPOT. DAY

Thomas and McLeary arrive at the works. A sign read "Mc Scotch Dairys 1920". The iron gates a gray haired bearded old night watchman of sixty years. He gives Thomas a salute and throws a doggie biscuits to McLeary. The Depot is busy, workers loading floats and moving pallets etc.

Thomas waves to some of them and checks the skies. "It's a cold one this morning, eh lads!" Some of the workers answer, agreeing and acknowledging McLeary, Thomas goes to his float, which is loaded and ready to go. He puts the ragdoll on the dashboard and goes around the float and checks off the manifest laying on top of the load, talking to McLeary throughout.

Thomas: "Okay, now what have we got here?" he mutters to himself

"42: Mrs. Grant, two pints and cream. Miss Jones wants some eggs that's grand. The butcher wants some fresh cheese, okay. It's all here. Right Laddie? Is you ready?"

Thomas and McLeary climb onto the float. McLeary settles into his place beside Thomas. Thomas starts up a light humming sound like a mass of bee's fills the air, Thomas drives out of the Depot in convoy with three other Blue, Milk Floats.

GLASGOW ROYAL INFIRMARY. EARLY DAY

The ambulance man hands Dr Love the note from the doctor Jamieson. Love slips it quickly into his top pocket.

Love to a Nurse: "Would you take care of Mrs. McKean, please?" Mary: "No. I want to stay with Hannah."

The nurse guides Mary towards the hospital Emergency entrance. Nurse: "She's in good hands. You just follow me."

With Mary gone, Love takes the paper from his pocket and reads it. As he takes in Doctor Jamieson's message, his expression changes perceptibly to concern and he watches as Hannah is wheeled inside.

THOMAS : BACK ON HIS MILK ROUND.

Thomas begins his delivery round and drops milk on the doorsteps of several houses.

At one house, he reads a note left in the top of a milk bottle.

Thomas: "Now, what do you think about that McLeary? Miss Lewes here wants an extra pint… be a good lad and fetch it for us."

McLeary gives a bark and goes to the back of the float, grabs a pint of milk in his teeth and takes it to Miss Lewes' step, placing it carefully beside the two pints.

Thomas has already delivered. He looks over from next door. Thomas: "Okay now. We'd better get a move on"

Together they get back on the milk float. As the float rounds a corner, Thomas hears a young boy cry out in pain.

Thomas stops and gets down, followed by McLeary. He looks down the back-end and sees the two youths, Smokey and Josh, beating up on Ian. Thomas, followed by McLeary runs toward them, barking.

Thomas is shouting at Josh and Smokey: "Lay off Ian you two." Josh turn to watch Thomas approaching.

Thomas: "Hey, you two, leave him alone he's only a half pint. Pick on someone your own size."

Smokey and Josh turn and face Thomas. Smokey pulls out a flick knife and waves it at Thomas.

Smokey: "Keep your nose out of this granddad, unless you want some of the same." Smokey starts to walk towards Thomas. He lets him get within striking distance and, with a speed which is unbelievable, at his age, straight arms Karate punch hit Smokey in the throat, leaving him gasping for breath on the ground, his flick knife lying in the gutter.

Josh goes toward the knife but McLeary is there before him, growling fiercely. Ian picks himself up. He has a bloody nose.

Smokey picks himself up: "You'll regret that you old eejit, if it's the last thing I do." Josh: "Aye. You won't always have your mutt with you.

Thomas: "There's no time like the present. OK? McLeary, up and at 'em boy"

As Josh comes right up to Thomas and tries to push him, he gets the same treatment Smokey got and McLeary, with a fierce growl launches himself at Smokey, who tears off up the road.

Thomas stands over Josh as McLeary rejoins him and is hugged by Ian.

Thomas: "Down, McLeary, down! Leave him!' Here lad, use this to wipe your nose Josh."

Josh: "You'd better watch yoursel' old man. You won't always have that bloody dog with you and we ain't finish with you"

McLeary backs off. Josh gets up.

Ian: "They sell drugs to some of the kids at school. If we don't buy they threaten to beat us up unless we pay them anyway."

Thomas: "Can't the teachers do something about it or the police?" Ian "The teachers don't want to. They're as scared of them as us".

Thomas: "Hmm. Maybe, we'll have to teach them a lesson? But, you're young Hannah's brother, Ian?" ....We already know that he knows he is her brother!!!!

Ian: "Aye. Pa's in hospital and now, Ma's going spare with worry."

Thomas: "Aye, I heard. Listen, m'lad, you get off home and clean yoursel' up.

McLeary and I've still got work to do.

Josh: "You'd better watch yoursel' Josh shout back at Thomas.

Ian: "Thanks, Mr McLeary and I'll get McLeary here, a bone from the butchers next time I see him. I'll tell the lads at school all about it."

Thomas (smiles): "He'll be your friend for life, you do that, but don't you go making more of it than there was. I've heard how you like to make a drama out of everything. Now, be off with you and give my regards to your Ma."

Ian turns and runs off.

Thomas and McLeary walk back to the milk float".

CHAPTER 5

GLASGOW ROYAL INFIRMARY

THE ECHO OFFICES.

The day has just begun. Jodie has just entered the office, when Stephen comes bursting in. Journalists and staff are working at their desks and making phone calls.

Stephen: "Okay. Listen up. Everyone stops what they are doing and pays attention. I've have just heard from a source at the hospital that policeman, Robert McKeen was admitted late last night with a gunshot wound whilst trying to stop a drug deal going down in the warehouse just of Dundee rd. The dealer was captured but his two accomplices escaped. Not only that, but the young girl who has been put into isolation is his daughter."

Stephen is walking around the office with a copy of the proof print in his hand. He approaches Jodie's workstation.

Stephen: "Now, the police won't let us near him yet but, there's not many kids put in isolation so quickly these days. So. John (a man in his late forties with a brown leather jacket and jean to match; looks like he just come off a night of boozes), you are covering the police angle. Oh, by the way, take young Jodie McFadden along with you. She knows the family and the mother will probably be glad to see a friendly face."

John is an old school, hard-bitten local journalist. He acknowledges the fact with a shrug: "Whatever". Stephen gives Jodie a smile.

Jodie: "Aye, I do know the McKeens. Nice family." Stephen: "Bring me back a real hard-hitting story, okay?"

John nods to Jodie as she looks across to Sam's desk. Sam gives her a huge grin and a thumb up.

GLASGOW ROYAL INFIRMARY - DAY

John drives up in his car, and parks. As Jodie goes to get out, he turns to her. John; "You just leave the talking to me, OK. Maybe you'll learn something?" Jodie (sweetly): "You won't even know I'm there, Mr McLone."

John and Jodie enter the hospital. John goes to the desk and tries to get to the front of the queue by showing his press card, and shouting "Press, Press" much to the annoyance of the waiting patients.

Sister Fay arrives.

Sister Faye: "Now, what's all the noise about?"

Jodie watches for a moment and seeing John, having got to the front, he seems to be arguing impatiently with the receptionist and the sister.

Jodie sees a sign: 'Children's Ward'. She heads towards it. There is a store cupboard marked 'Staff only'. She opens the door. Inside are cleaning materials and a white coat on a peg. Jodie grabs the coat and slips it on and reemerges into the corridor. John is still at the desk and is getting nowhere.

CHILDREN'S WARD DAY

The ward is busy. It is visiting time. Jodie walks among the parents and children looking for Hannah's bed. A staff doctor and a nurse pass her without comment. Jodie cannot see Hannah anywhere. Two nurses pass.

Nurse 1: "Oh. The poor wee thing. Only this morning you say?"

Nurse 2: "Aye. Doctor Love put her straight into the isolation ward. That's not good news. I'm afraid we'll be seeing a lot more of her?"

Jodie sees the sign 'isolation ward' above the door at the end of the corridor and walks towards it. Another door marked 'geriatric ward', half glass is at the end. She reaches the 'Isolation Ward' door and sees Dr. Love talking to Mary beside Hannah's bed. Hannah is hooked up to various drips and machines. Mary is in tears. As Jodie peers through the glass she is surprised by a tap on the shoulder. Jodie spins around to face with a little old man with a Zimmer frame.

Old Man: "Doctor Can you tell me where to go for my enema?" Jodie thinking on her feet: "You'd better ask the charge nurse. Bye" Jodie turns and briskly walks back through the children's ward.

ROYAL INFIRMARY - RECEPTION

There is another Receptionist behind the desk and John is busy chatting her up. A big smile crosses his face as he leans on the front desk.

John: "So, my beauty I hear a policeman was brought in early this morning with gunshot wounds? Maybe we could have a wee bit of lunch and you tell me all about it?"

John pats her hand conspiratorially across the desk which she angrily withdraws and turns to the next person in the queue. John quietly fumes as he looks for Jodie who is no- where to be seen.

Thomas's FLAT.

Thomas returns from his round. McLeary follows him into the kitchen and watches keenly as Thomas prepares him some food, putting his paws on the table as Thomas opens the tin off dog food. Thomas pats him.

Thomas: "Well. McLeary! Taken away in an ambulance, hey? What do you think? I'll have a wee word with Doctor Jamieson today. I'll see if I can find out a bit more about Hanna from him.

Thomas puts McLeary's bowl on the floor. Thomas: "There ye go, boy. Eat it up."

McLeary's digs in. Thomas makes a cup of tea and a sandwich and exits the kitchen.

THE ECHO - EDITOR'S OFFICES. DAY.

Jodie and John are in Stephen's office. Stephen is sitting back in his chair talking on the phone. There are pictures on the walls of Stephen with well-known people and celebrities. On his desk is a pile of cuttings and two other phones.

Stephen: "What. No. I said today. or you'll be hearing from my lawyer."

Stephen slams down the phone. Jodie looks at John who has a note pad in his hand. Stephen: "Well, John. Spill"

John reads from his notes.

John: "I quizzed one of the Doctors but they're not saying much apart from the fact that he's in intensive care on account of gunshot wounds but it's only a precautionary measure and the girl's just in for observation".

Stephen: "Closing ranks eh?"

John nods as Jodie raises her hand.

Stephen: "Yes. Miss. McFadden. School's over now!"

Jodie, embarrassed: "I don't think that's quite true, sir. I saw, a doctor talking to Mrs. McKeen. I couldn't hear what was said but it looked serious. The Doctor, is a Doctor Love a leading pediatrician. I mean, she's in an Isolation ward with all sorts of equipment attached to her. I'd say it is more than just observation"

Stephen: "Well done. That's great. How did find all this out?"

Jodie: "Well. I pinched a white coat from a store cupboard and pretended to be staff."

Stephen: "OK. OK. I get the picture. That shows initiative"

John, defensively: "I'd have got around to it! I was interested in the copper and the shooting"

Stephen, ignoring him: "Okay, Jodie. The girl's story's yours. Don't let me down." John looks sideways at Jodie. Jodie's beaming smile is so big she doesn't notice. Jodie: "I'll try not to Stephen."

John and Jodie leave Stephen who picks up the phone.

As Jodie and John come out of Stephen's office, John takes Jodie by the arm and stands her against the wall.

THE ECHO PRESS OFFICES. DAY.

John: "Okay, Miss Marple's. Just listen up and mark my words. You think you've done well, don't you?"

Jodie stares hard at John.

John: "It takes more than nicking a white coat and listening behind closed doors to make a reporter. You'll see. Just you wait"

Jodie is about to reply when Stephen comes out of his office, carrying some papers.

He realizes that they've had words.

"Come on Jodie" Stephen says: "go, go".

Stephen: "John. Come with me. You concentrate on the police angle"

They walk off down the corridor. Jodie overhears the conversation and smiles. Stephen: "Now in hell's name is this? G M crops not for locals! Either's this story!

This is not a local rag for the Women's Union - my jobs to get this rag to a National level. No more parochial stuff. Now get your ass into gear and think National."

Thomas's FLAT.

Thomas settles into his chair his glasses at the end of this nose, he start reading his new book. McLeary is chewing on a 'dog chew'. Thomas closes the book and taps the picture on the front.

Thomas: "Do you know, McLeary? Jock Lewes, myself and your grandfather walked for miles without water for days to prove a point."

McLeary looks up at Thomas and barks. Thomas glances at the clock.

Thomas: "Oh, my, look at the time. Come on or we're going to be late for the Doctor…"

ISOLATION WARD GLASGOW ROYAL

Hanna is still very pale and ill. Many monitors surround the drip that is by her bed and she is hooked up to an oxygen ventilator. Mary sits holding Hannah's hand and stroking her hair. Dr. Love enters with a file under his arm.

Love: "Mrs. McKeen. Here are the preliminary results. I had hoped I could give you some better news, but as it is, I'm sorry"

Mary, agonized: "Hannah's not going to die? Don't tell me that!"

Love: "I didn't say that but she is going to need special treatment which is expensive."

Mary gets up indignant.

Mary: "That's a young girl lying there. My daughter and all you can talk about is expense. I thought this was a hospital not a pawnshop."

Love: "Please, Mrs. McKeen, I understand your anger and I'm pulling out all the stops to get Hannah the help she needs. Hannah has rare form of leukemia."

Mary: "What's that?"

Love: "It's a form of cancer but, at her age and the fact that we've diagnosed it so early, if we can find a donor with the same blood group as Hannah, she's got a great chance of a full recovery.

Mary: "I don't understand it. One minute she's playing about with her friends and the next she's here, wired up like something out of a horror film."

Love: "Mrs McKeen. Your husband's off the danger list. He's working with an Identikit artist to try and visualize the man who shot him and the two men who got away."

Love's pager goes off. Love picks up the house phone in Hanna room. "Love here. OK I'll be right there. Remember, we do have chance."

Mary: "Chances, he says! It sounds more like a miracle she'll be needing."

Love: "Doctors don't believe in miracles Mrs. McKeen, but, for once in my life I hope that a miracle will happen. I'll explain later"

Love exits as Mary strokes Hannah's forehead, saying. Mary: "Sweet angels "please help my wee child.

DOCTOR JAMESON'S SURGERY

Doctor Jamieson is making notes as Thomas enters. There is a couch behind a screen and a glass fronted medical cabinet containing instruments and medical supplies On the old wooden desk with a dark red leather a number of case files drawing hanging on the wall of medical stuff and a picture framed, including Jameson's young daughter.

The doctor looks to Thomas and covers the mouthpiece with his hand. Doesn't want Thomas to know what he saying.

Jamieson: "Take the weight off your plates. Thomas, I won't be a minute" Jamieson exits. Thomas smiles and sits down. The doctor returns to his phone call.

Jamieson: "I see, well so, what's next doctor Love? I'm glad I got her to you when I did. Nationwide, you say? That'll take some organizing. OK. We'll speak later."

The doctor replaces the handset and takes up Thomas's file.

Jamieson: "Thomas. You're looking healthy enough. I hope you're not wasting my time."

Thomas: "So do I, Jamie, but, I'm more worried about young Hannah McKeen."

Jamieson: "Aye, and so you should be, but, ye ken, I cannae discuss another patient. Friend or no. But go get your breeks (trousers) down and I'll give you a quick examination."

Thomas goes behind a screen, while Jamieson picks up the phone.

THE ECHO PRESS OFFICES.

Jodie is at her desk looking at her typewriter when Sam looks over. Sam places a Cadbury walnut whip in front of her. Jodie doesn't move.

Sam: "Cadburys' calling Jodie McFadden! It's Walnut Whip time. Come in McFadden!

Time is up."

Jodie comes back to senses and smiles. Jodie: "Thanks".

Sam: "You've really done it, haven't you? The world's your oyster now, my girl. Just don't forget your old mates along the way. I knew you could do it."

Jodie: "I'm learning. You know what they say. Beware of what you want in case you get it"

Sam: "Rubbish. With your brains and looks, all you needed was a wee bit of luck." Jodie: "I've already made an enemy of that: John McLone. He didn't take kindly to my upstaging him with Hannah McKeen."

Sam: "Och, he's just a jealous old eejit". She counts on her fingers "Has he got your looks? No! Does he have your brains? No! Does he have womanly wiles? No! Put those three together, he's a three-time loser."

Jodie: "But, he does have experience. To be a good reporter, you can't just rely on luck. You have to know your subject matter and the background."

Sam: "Aye I suppose that does enter the equation, but you've got a head start." Jodie: "That's why I'm going to see that Mrs. McKeen as soon as I can.

Luckily, she lives in the same back-end as we do."

Sam: "That's not going to be easy. With her daughter the way she is and her husband. Having been show."

Jodie: "That's true but, I have a wee idea."

DOCTOR JAMESON'S WAITING ROOM.

Thomas is by the reception desk when the phone rings. Receptionist answers.

Receptionist: "Surgery. Good afternoon can I help you? Oh Doctor Love our put you straight through". The Receptionist presses the phone button.

Receptionist: "Thomas. Just hold the fort for a minute would you, be a love, I'm bursting."

The Receptionist quickly scuttles off. Thomas can hear the muffled conversation on the phone. He glances around. There is no-one about so he leans over and turns up the volume on the speakerphone.

Jamieson's voice: "could be a form, of Leukemia? That's not good news". Love's voice: "No. The only solution is the donor"

Jamieson's voice: "Good God! That's a hellish expensive option and time consuming. Is there no other way?"

Love: "I know of only two specialists in the field. One is in London, private practice and very expensive. The other is out of the question, he's in the US."

Jamieson is silent, taking this in as Thomas hears the look flush. Jamieson: "How is she doing so far?"

Love: "Holding her own but that may not last forever!"

The Receptionist opens the door just as Thomas is turning the sound back down and spinning to face her as innocently as he can.

Receptionist: "I'm sorry about that Thomas."

Thomas: "Nae bother when you've got tae go you've got to go."
Receptionist (smiles): "How right you are, Thomas."

KITCHEN. EVENING

Jodie bursts through the door. Alice is at the sink washing up. She turns around with a bowl and a sponge in her hands. Jodie is feigning sadness.

Alice: "Jodie, what is it, pet?"

Jodie grins from ear to ear and sits down at the table Alice puts away the bowl and pours a cup tea from the from the pot on the table. Jodie lights a cigarette.

Jodie: "I've got it Mum. My first assignment. All my very own." Alice: "That wonderful Jodie...what's it about?

Jodie: "Not so wonderful Mum? It's Mary McKeen's little girl Hannah. She was admitted to hospital, just after her father came out of surgery having been shot in a drugs raid early this morning. That old reporter, John McLone, and I were sent down to follow up on that story about three shootings of her father"

Jodie takes a gulp of tea. Alice sits opposite with a fag and her own cup of tea.

Jodie: "Mr.McLone tried the big I am reporter bit whilst I did a bit of investigating on my own. You know, human interest. I overheard two nurses talking about Hannah and how she's very poorly and she'd be there for some time. I pinched a white coat and got into the children's ward"

She pauses and puffs on her cigarette.

"She's in an Isolation Ward. I took a peek through the glass and saw a Doctor talking to Mary. Oh, Mum it was terrible. This wee girl like in a Jam jar. She was crying fit to burst."

Alice takes a puff and flicks ash into the ashtray. Alice: "Could you hear what they were saying?"

Jodie shakes her head: "Whatever it was, it was not good and the doctor, a Doctor Love, is the top man with kids, it sounded very serious."

Alice: "Certainly sounds serious. And then?"

Jodie: "An old boy crept up behind me and tapped me on the shoulder." Jodie giggles: "I nearly wee myself"

Alice: "Ooh!"

Jodie still giggling: "Yeah, but then he asked me where to go for his enema…" Alice: "His what?"

Jodie: "Enema you know?" With a coy gesture up the bum. Alice: "He didn't want you to do it?"

Jodie: "Don't! No Ma. I just told him to see the charge nurse and bolted!" Alice: "So what happen next?"

Jodie winks: "Same time, same channel, tomorrow. Stay tuned Ma… What's for supper, I'm fair starving and I'm off to the pub with Sam in a wee while"

Thomas's FLAT. EVENING

Thomas is sitting in his chair cleaning his medals. On the table is a tin of polish and a plate on which is a part eaten slice of cake. McLeary is sleeping. Thomas pauses in his work and glances at the clock. His gaze is held for a second by the picture beside it of Thomas and the officer Lt McFadden he saved in the desert with McLeary's great grandfather. His eyes fall to the book on the chest just below and then to McLeary. Thomas claps his hands and wakes McLeary.

Thomas: "Come on lad. It's time we took our evening run."

McLeary gets up and shakes himself. Thomas stands, slips off his slippers and goes to the door and puts on pair of tattered running shoes.

JODIE'S ROOM EVENING

Jodie is at her electric typewriter, a prize for becoming young journalist of the year and is beginning to write Hannah's story.

Jodie writing as she talks: "Time line 5.30 am: Young girl admitted to Glasgow Royal. Hannah McKeen, 4, was admitted to the Glasgow Royal Infirmary early yesterday morning where, only a day before her father, PC McKeen had been admitted with gunshot wounds sustained whilst trying to arrest a drug dealer.

PC McKeen is recovering well but the hospital is running a series of tests to establish why Hannah, who is in the Isolation Ward, is being kept under close observation?"

The door opens and Alice enters with her supper and a cup of tea on a tray Alice: "Now, my girl. You cannot work on an empty stomach."

Jodie: "Och, Mum. It's my story and it has to be in by tomorrow morning" Alice peers over her shoulder and reads silently.

Alice: "Well, that's a fine start.

Jodie: "Aye, but it's really hard. That's my fifth attempt. I've heard of Robert the Bruce but this is ridiculous"

Alice quietly says: "Just write it like you were talking to me.

Jodie is beaver- ring at the typewriter. The finger touches each key Jodie starts to grin, her food is untouched on the tray beside her.

CHAPTER 6

EVENING RUN

THOMAS'S HAZE OF STREET LIGHT

Thomas and McLeary begin to jog steadily along the street. In the background, hidden behind a truck, Smokey and Josh stand watching him.

Smokey: "I'm nae goin' (not going) near him with that bloody dog on his heels."

Josh: "Aye, we've got tae (time), think about how to deal with him. Let's see what he's up to."

They follow Thomas and McLeary at a safe distance.

THE PARK BENCH. EVENING

Susan Wilson, a nurse from the Glasgow Royal, dressed all ready to a second shift, and old friend of Thomas -she stitched Thomas up when he fell out of his cab on a winter December day- and McLeary are sitting chatting on a park bench. Smokey and Josh are in the background. Watching and waiting.

Thomas: "So what can you tell me about young Hannah McKeen?" Susan: "Susan I'm not sure I should be telling you anything?" Thomas: "Come on my girl. Who am I going to tell."

Susan: "It's look like leukemia"

Thomas: "That's awful. Is there no a cure?" Susan: "Aye, there is today but she needs blood.

Thomas: "If I thought it would do any good, I could volunteer the blood but I think it might just have a tad too much of the malt in it"

Susan: "I can believe that but you're not. Even if we had a donor the cost is astronomical.

Thomas: "What astronomical".

Susan: "More than fifty thousand pounds." Thomas: "Aye - that's a tidy sum, right enough."

Susan: "Yes and, apart from that, the doctors say, at the outside, she's only got about a month."

Thomas: "That's no time at all and I don't think the McKeen's' would have that sort of money around the house, not on a copper's pay. He's lying in the same hospital, shot in the line of duty. Like many of my old mates."

Susan: "During the war?"

Thomas: "Aye. S.A.S. but for Hannah, she'll not see Christmas, nor another birthday come to that. Aye?"

Susan: "You know, I sometimes wonder too is there really a good God." A church clock strikes the half hour.

Susan: "Well, I have to go. I'm on shift in twenty minutes and Matron's a stickler for time. You both take care."

Susan strokes McLeary's head and gets up. Thomas gets up too.

Thomas: "Aye, it's late. Shall I run you to the gate, just to be on the safe side?" Susan: "That would be nice. Thanks."

Thomas: "Come on McLeary. We've a job to do."

Susan grins. McLeary barks and does not want to move.

Thomas: "McLeary, come on, we're on escort duty. Sorry Susan. He's not usually so slow"

As Susan jogs off, Thomas looks round as McLeary looks back into the park. Smokey and Josh come out from hiding standing under a broken lamp watching them Smokey: "We can wait. There'll be other nights."

They slope off into the darkness and down to the pub where Sam is.

THE PUB. NIGHT

Sam is outside the pub at a table with three friends. Sam looks at her watch and goes to a nearby phone booth. She dials. Waits and replaces the receiver.

There is no reply. Jodie is asleep at her type writer.

THE ECHO PRESS OFFICES

Jodie is outside Stephen's door with her copy. Stephen comes up the stairs. John is behind him but stops as he hears Stephen.

Stephen: "Morning Jodie. What's that I spies?"

Jodie: "I've got the first part of the Hannah McKeen story but I have an idea for a follow up."

Stephen: "Okay, fine, I'd love to hear it. Come in and tell me about it. It better be good"

Stephen and Jodie go into Stephen's office as John comes up the stairs. John then go down the hallway to the Men's.

John, under his breath: "You ass-licking bitch".

THE MILK DEPOT.

Milk floats come and go. The depot is busy. Thomas has returned from his round. Thomas unloads the empty crates. McLeary is lapping up some milk that Thomas has given him.

GLASGOW GRAND CENTRAL STATION

A newspaper seller is selling papers carrying headline on the front page: "POLICE SHOT -see inside Get Your Newspaper. Here Read all about it POLICE MAN SHOT IN THE LINE OF DUTY"

PRINT SHOP

Thomas enters the print shop. The printing press makes a sound like steam engine. On the counter are a pile of different colure paper and card and envelopes. A young boy Austin is busy at the counter. A copier is working full tilt in background.

Austin: "Hi Thomas. How are you?"

Thomas: "I'm fine, young Austin. I've a question. You know yon leaflet things they keep sticking through my letterbox."

Austin: "Aye! You mean flyers?"

Thomas: "Aye. That's them. Can anyone do them and how much do they cost?" Austin: "Depends on how many you want."

Thomas: "Well. How many have there milk delivered around here do you think?" Austin: "If it's advertising, you have to pay more. What would they be for?"

Thomas: "I need to spread a wee word."

Austin: "Oh. So, you're not thinking of starting a national campaign then?" Thomas: "No. Just for the folks around about."

Austin: "Well. Why don't you start with a five hundred we can always print more if you need them?"

Thomas: "As you say. Seems an awful lot. How much would that be?"

Austin: "I'll ask my Pa. Seeing as it's you, I'm sure he'll give you a discount if it's for a good cause. Will you be back?"

HANNAS'S WARD GLASGOW ROYAL

Hannah is semi-conscious. Mary is beside Hannah's bed and is reading to her from a book, one of a Fairy Story novel. Dr Love enters the room.

Mary: "I hope you've some good news? I can't take much more of this. You haven't told her Da', I hope?"

Love: "No, we haven't informed P C. McKeen. As far as Hannah's concerned its good news and bad Mrs. McKeen. As I said the difficulty is finding the right donor and in time."

Love hesitates - he coughs

Mary: "Come on man. Out with it..."

Love: "Well. I'm sorry. It's also a question of administration."

Mary: "By administration I assume you mean money? The bloody system. I thought The National Health Service was for the nation, not only for those across the border."

Love tries to speak. Mary cuts him off.

Mary: "You people... you're all the bloody same. Look at her. Are you going to tell me there's a price on that wee barn's' head, like that druggie who shot her Da' yesterday!"

Love: "Mrs. McKeen. If I could do myself, her and now, I would, believe me. We have to wait for a donor and that's not a matter of money. We're supposed to be experts, but which God appointed us?"

Love goes to Mary and puts his hands on her shoulders and gives a gently squeeze, turns and leaves. A Nurse checks Hannas' support system. Mary sits down wearily.

THOMAS'S KITCHEN.

Thomas is poring over a map of the UK. He traces a red line marking out a route from Glasgow Central Station to Southern Scotland. Nearby is a plate of food that Thomas picks at as he works. The S.A.S. book is on the table. There is washing up in the sink. McLeary is nearby.

Thomas: "Mr. McLeary. You and I, we're going to take a wee walk"

He continues the line of the route right the way down to Land's End. McLeary puts his front paws onto the map and barks and wags his tail excitedly.

THE ECHO PRESS OFFICES

As Jodie arrives for work Stephen's voice booms through the building. John passes her on the stairs.

Stephen voice: "Jodie!" John hears this and smiles wickedly at Jodie, thinking she is in trouble. Jodie ignores him and continues up the stairs.

THE PRINT SHOP. DAY

Thomas enters the shop with McLeary. Austin's father Mr. Lewis, a short fat inkling of man and Austin greet him. Thomas has the draft of his flyer in his hand and he puts it onto the counter.

Lewis: "Morning Thomas. What have ye there?"

Thomas: "It's for one of yon flyers I was talking about with young Austin." Lewis: "Okay, let's have a wee look."

Lewis pick up the flyer and examines it. On the top of the flyer is a picture of Hannah with her arms around McLeary's neck. Below that is the insignia of the S.A.S. and it's motto.

"Who Dares Wins"

The message reads:

"WALKING FOR HANNAH'S LIFE

Mr. McLeary and I will re-enact a walk I did with his Grandfather twenty years ago during the war.

The war is now over the majority of us but Hannah's fight has just begun. She has death tapping on her door.

She needs a donor and funds to pay for the Specialist to save her life. PLEASE HELP"

Below the message is a diagrammatic outline of the route march from Glasgow Central to Lands' End.

Lewis puts down the FLYER and leans on both fists on the counter. Thomas takes out his wallet and removes a small wad of money and asks uncertainly:

Thomas: "Will that be expensive?"

Lewis: "Put your money away, Thomas. What can I say? No charge."

Thomas: "You're a good man Lewis McDermott. I hope there are many more like you. God knows she's going to need them."

Lewis picks up the flyer again.

Lewis: "There will be, Thomas, there will be. Pop by in a couple of hours. Young Austin's going to the motocross tomorrow afternoon, he can take a bunch and put them about"

Thomas smiles his thanks. McLeary barks.

THE ECHO PRESS. STEPHEN'S OFFICE. DAY.

Stephen is pacing the floor and talking into the phone which he replaces as Jodie enter the offices.

Jodie: "Stephen. You wanted me? Sorry, I just had to add a bit to what I wrote last night. Have you had a look at the draft?"

Stephen: "Yes, I have - and you've earned yourself a follow up piece. Tomorrow.

Same Time. Same Place"

Jodie: "Oh that's great. And did you have a chance to think about the other idea.

The appeal?"

Stephen: "Let's look at that later, eh?" Jodie: "Okay. Grand!"

Jodie leaves the office as Stephen picks up the phone.

Stephen: "Dougie, as I told you, I think we've a little gem here. Name's Jodie McFadden. Bright as a new pin. She's got an idea I want to run by you."

MILK DEPOT EARLY.

The Milk Depot is busy as usual. Thomas has a bundle of flyers and a bag of elastic bands. He is attaching a single flyer to each bottle on his deliveries with the elastic bands. Another milkman (Gary) tall a skinny, much younger, with a roll up fags dangle from the side of his mouth come over. Thomas with a white coat and a blue wooly hat and scarf.

Thomas: "Morning, Gary! Still!"

Gary: "What have you got there, Thomas?" Thomas is reticent.

Gary: "Come on. Knowing you, it'll no be a bit of business for yourself. Hand, it over."

Thomas hands Gary a flyer. Gary reads it.

Gary: "Why were you keeping this to yourself?" Gary calls out to the nearby Milkmen.

Gary: "Okay you guys. Gather round here a minute" Thomas tries to stop Gary.

Gary: "Nay Thomas, this is something special. It involves us all especially with her Da' being in hospital as well."

The Milkmen assemble around Gary. Thomas is to one side, by his float.

Gary: "It seems like we have a message in a bottle. We'll all to take a leaflet or two from Thomas here and do what he's doing."

Thomas: "You guys are too much – thanks."

Gary: "What you're doing is a good thing, Thomas. A regular Knight in shining armor.

I hear you beat up a gang of thug's a while back?"

Thomas: "Well won't say beat up. Ian McKeen. He lets his imagination run riot." Gary: "That's for sure. How many were there? Ten, twenty"

Thomas: "Away with you. They were two young Skellums. Nae bother for an old hand like me."

Gary: "Anyway, we should be giving you a hand. When are you planning to start?"

Thomas: "Well. I've got some holiday due so, I'm hoping to be off by the weekend which is a long one. Should be plenty people out and about. I've not got long to do it."

Gary: "Lands' End! That's an awful long way. You'll have to do about thirty miles a day?"

Thomas: "I know Gary, but you see. I feel a need to save her. I've known her since she was a wain (baby). I've done it before! With a good wind, I just might do it." Gary: "That was a few good years ago."

Thomas: "I'd still give you a run for your money, you cheeky young sod." Gary, Laughing: "We're all with you aren't we lads?"

The Milkmen, cheer and bee there horn head back to their floats.

HANNAS'S WARD. GLASGOW ROYAL

The room is still as all we hear are the machines there whispering sounds of death as we see young Hanna. Eyes are shut. Mary is in a chair. Hannah is asleep on the bed, still wired up. Several 'Get Well' cards are around the room, a number of soft toys are by her side and on Hanna bedside table are some flowers, with messages. Get well cards cover her room and soft toys all different shapes and sizes.

CHILDREN'S WARD

Susan is walking quietly away from the 'Isolation Ward', checking on the sleeping children. the sleeping children. There is a sudden sound from the direction of Hannah's Ward. Susan stops, turns and briskly walks towards it. She goes through the door into the Ward and looks around. Mary and Hannah are still fast asleep, but now, Hannah's rag doll lies on the bedside table. Wrapped around is a flyer tied with a beautiful pink boo.

GLASGOW STREET. EARLY

Street houses all have milk bottles on the doorsteps with fliers attached. Inhabitants come out of their doors. Women are in there night dresses and others dressed for a brand new day. There is a breeze and a few drops of morning rain. They are picking up their milk and taking it inside, some read the flyer before going in. Old man news-seller at the corner cuts open a bundle of papers.

The headline reads "Young Girl Fights for Life: Appeal…See inside story"

Some people come and buy, and some, looking at the headline which is pasted on the newspapers stand as they pass by, mutter together with their folks.

LOCAL CORNER SHOP. MID MORNING

Thomas enters the shop, carrying an ancient army issue rucksack. McLeary waits outside. Mrs Argent, an old Indian shopkeeper, dressed in a greenie-blue Sari greets Thomas, who has a piece of paper in his hand. There is a pack of flyers on the counter.

Mrs Argent: "Morning Thomas"

Thomas: "Aye, it's grand morning Mrs Argent! I'll be needing some rations for my trip."

Thomas hands Mrs Argent the piece of paper.

Mrs Argent (nods at the flier): "This is quite a list, Thomas. Leave it with me, I'll put it together for you. And a bar of chocolate for McLeary and you.

THE ECHO PRESS OFFICES.

In the tearoom, Sam is with some friends. Sam is making tea and the friends are smoking. Jodie bursts in, holding a flier. She goes over and grabs one cup of tea. She shows it to Sam.

Jodie: "Have you seen this?"

Sam: "No. What is it, some major rave?"

Jodie: "Is that all you think about Sammie McCaskill ? Guy Thomas and his dog McLeary... they're going to do a charity walk from Grand Central Station to Land's End."

Sam: "For that wee girl, Hannah, in hospital I hear about that this morning"

Jodie goes towards a seat and lights a cigarette. John has entered and waits before he goes to the coffee table ignoring the girls.

Jodie: "Aye. I'm going to ask Stephen if I can go with them. Report the story along the way."

Sam: "Jodie McFadden! You can't walk from Glasgow to Land's End... You've a job walking to the head of your stairs."

Jodie: "No, silly. I'll be in a car, they're doing the walking. I'll just phone back the story to Steve as they go."

John takes his time over making his coffee. He takes a slow sip before turning and walking back out of the tearoom. He has a self-satisfied smile on his face.

Sam and Jodie exchange glances as the door swings shut Sam: "Oh. It's 'Steve' now is it?"

Jodie: "You don't think he heard do you?"

Sam: "Not sure but you watch that one, Jodie. He's after you and I don't mean your body. It's your blood. Jodie I'd better go and see Stephen right now after you've been to the little girl's room."

MRS ARGENT'S SHOP.

Thomas rucksack is on the floor. On the counter is a huge pile of shopping. Mrs Argent is barely visible at the till. A woman enters the shop and hands Thomas an envelope. Thomas looks inside.

Woman: "Thomas. It's not much, but I want you to have it for wee Hannah." Inside the envelope a couple-pound notes.

Thomas: "You're a good woman. I thank you... and Mr. McLeary thanks you as well"

The woman smiles and leaves the shop. The till rings as Mrs Argent gets the final total.

Mrs Argent: "It comes to a tidy sum, Thomas?".

Thomas: "Aye, I would think it would come to quite a bit. Okay. What's the damage?"

Mrs Argent beckons Thomas to come closer. Thomas is quizzical. Mrs Argent beckons again as Thomas takes out his wallet. Thomas leans close to her, cocking an ear. Mrs Argent looks Thomas squarely in the eye.

Mrs Argent: "The till doesn't seem to have woken up yet, now I wonder why?" She gives Thomas a wink.

INT THE ECHO - EDITOR'S

Jodie enters Stephen's office. John is standing there with a supercilious grin on his face and a flyer in his hand.
dog.
Stephen: "John's just told me of this great idea of his about this man Thomas and his
Jodie: "But sir…!"
John: "Jodie. A good reporter never gives away a good story, even to friends" Stephen: "You wanted to say something, Jodie?"
Jodie: "No. Not for the moment"
Stephen: "Well. No matter. I have decided to put both of you on this story. John drives, you don't! And it would be a learning curve for you to be with a good reporter.
John: "I'm sure it's a one-man job, Stephen. Old soldiers and all that. Man, to man"
Stephen: "John, I'm not sure you were even in the Boy-Scouts? These flyers are in public domain. It was Jodie's intuition that brought it to us and with your experience, this is just the sort of story that can put this paper on the National stands first. Let the others try and catch us."
John: "You're the governor, Stephen."
Stephen: "That's right. Listen, if you don't want the assignment, just say so." John, angry: "I wasn't employed to be a chauffeur."
He storms out of the office. Stephen ignores the tantrum. Jodie: "Maybe it would be better if"
Stephen: "Jodie. Forget it. A few drams and he'll be OK. I had hunch it was your idea in the first place. You get your butt around to this McLeary chap."

Jodie: "But, I made an appointment with Mary McKeen. Nae-one got her side of the story yet."

Stephen: "Trust a woman to think of that. OK. You do that and then go and see McLeary."

THOMAS'S FLAT

Thomas is outside his door. The full rucksack is on his back and he is carrying four full carrier bags. McLeary carries another bag. Thomas puts down the carriers, unlocks the door and tries to open it. The door sticks. Thomas shoves on the door half open. On the floor is pile envelopes that have jammed it.

As McLeary scuttles inside, Thomas moves the envelopes enough to get in and follows McLeary in. Inside, Thomas drops the carrier bags and slips off his rucksack. Picking up a handful of envelopes, he opens one.

Thomas: "Well, well, well, McLeary ! This one's for wee Hannah! All for Hanna...Nope this one is a gas bill"

THE ECHO PRESS OFFICES

John storms out of the office building and marches across the forecourt to his car. He wrenches open the car door, slams himself into the driving seat and ram the car into gear, starts cursing and banging his hand on the steering wheel, starts up, revving hard. He spins the wheels as he drives away fast.

THOMAS'S FLAT

On the kitchen table, the carrier bags and the rucksack are unopened. His letterbox makes a sound as more letters come falling on to his mat.

Thomas gazes from the kitchen. He is sitting in his chair surrounded by opened envelopes at his feet. He is amazed.

Thomas: "Well. I'd never believe it. They're all made out either to the hospital or in aid of Hannah. I think we should be postmen for the day?"

CHAPTER 7

SO, IT BEGINS

Thomas and McLeary arrive on foot at the hospital. As a number of people are coming in and out. Thomas is carrying all the envelopes tied with an elastic band. He leashes up McLeary outside and goes in.

GLASGOW ROYAL

A bus stops outside the Glasgow Royal. Jodie alights and goes across to the hospital and sees McLeary tethered up. She goes inside and watches as Thomas approaches the Receptionist.

RECEPTION DESK GLASGOW ROYAL

Thomas walks up to the reception desk.

Receptionist looks up. Thomas drops the bundle of envelopes on the counter in front of her. The Receptionist eyes him suspiciously.

Thomas: "Would you be good enough to give these to that Doctor that's looking after wee Hannah McKeen"

Receptionist: "I can't just take these. Who are you?"

Receptionist (cont.): "What right have you got to just walk in here and dump all these envelopes on my desk. This is a hospital not a sorting office for the postal service and I'm not a postman"

Jodie steps forward, indignant.

Jodie: "And neither is Mr McLeary here. He's a milkman with a difference. He's got a heart. Come on Mr.McLeary. We've got a dog waiting."

With that she grabs Thomas's arm and they walk out of the hospital, leaving an astounded receptionist looking at the pile of mail inching her head.

Jodie and Thomas come out of the hospital, unleash McLeary and walk towards the bus stop.

Susan walks through the reception area and, as she passes the reception desk, she notices the piles of envelopes. She picks one up and sees Hannah's name on a few of them.

Susan: "What are all these doing? Shouldn't Doctor Love see these, Glade?"

Receptionist, grumpily: "I'm paid to look after the desk, not to play postman's knock."

Susan: "I don't think that doing a sick patient favors would qualify as gallivanting but seeing as you're overloaded with work, I'll make sure they get to the right person."

Taking the pile of envelopes, she turns and walks away unaware of the two-fingered gesture the receptionist has given her behind her back.

MOTOCROSS TRACK.

Roar of twenty motocross bikes as they rev up at the start of a race at a Glasgow motocross track. A bike skids in as they maneuver in and out. sounds of the noise of the bikes as they jump over the course echo. On-lookers cheer at the track side with rapturous enthusiasm and anticipation as the race comes to an end. There is a festival atmosphere with stalls selling everything from sweets to motor bike spares. Among an excited Ian munches on a hot dog.

At the hotdog stall, Smokey and Josh stand apart eating a hotdog as well. A young boy is on the ground, holding on to his bloody nose from being smacked earlier by Josh because he has not been selling enough stuff. Josh has taken over and sells drugs to an assortment of customers, whilst Smokey keeps a look out for the police.

The race having finished, Ian joins the queue for a hotdog and watches as Austin pastes one of the flyers on the side of the hot-dog stall. Josh walks over to see what it says. Ian catches sight of him and ducks out of sight behind the stall. He is about to walk away when he hears Josh speaking with Smokey. He listens intently.

Josh: "See this, Smokey?" Smokey: "What is it?"

Josh: "That old git(man) with the dog. Reckons he's going tae walk to Lands' End." Smokey: "What the hell for?"

Josh: "Collecting money for some kid in hospital. What say we follow him and when he's got enough dosh, there might be some sort of accident. Look, he's even given us the map"

while"

Josh put one in his pocket hand the other to Smokey, grinning at each other. Ian listens to their plans and is horrified.

Smokey: "You reckon he'll be good for a few bob after a couple of days." Josh: "Sure to be. Pay us back for that bloody dog that attacked us."

Smokey: "Yeah, and we'll be able to pay off the Big Yun - get him off our backs for a

Josh: "Shouldn't be too difficult. Just have to watch out for that bloody dog" Smokey: "Nae problem. We'll get some meat and put some rat poison on it." Josh: "Then we knock the old man out, right?"

He looks at the flyer and tears it into little pieces.

Smokey: "Right on, me old china. This piece of sheit is going to give us a good pay day. Nae problem."

The two youths walk away and Ian emerges from behind the hotdog stall. Looks around and, making sure that he is not seen, gazes down at the pieces of paper, then hurries off into the crowd.

THOMAS'S BUILDING. LATE

Jodie and Thomas step off the bus outside their tenement building. It is beginning to rain. Thomas gestures for Jodie to follow him in.

Thomas: "Come away in, Jodie McFadden. What on earth were you doing at the hospital?"

Jodie: "I'd come to interview Mrs. McKeen and was then coming to see you but, when that snooty bitch started, I thought, I can always see her tomorrow and you were cornered. I wanted to talk to you about your walk. Is that OK"?

Thomas: "Having come to my rescue, I can hardly say no. Come on in, I'll brew us some tea there some Dundee cake. Maybe the rain will have stopped by then?"

ROYAL INFIRMARY - DR LOVE'S OFFICE

Dr Love is busy behind his desk going through some papers Susan, knocked on the door, enters with her pile of letters.

Doctor Love: "What on earth have you got there, Nurse? Are we that short staffed that nurses have to go delivering the mail now?"

Susan: "No, sir, but I thought you should be aware of all the attention we're getting about Hannah. I hope you don't mind?"

Doctor Love: "Mind! Mind! Of course, I mind Nurse. I'm a doctor. This has become more than just duty. I'm not a loser. "A" should stand for assistance, not damned Administration"

He looks at Susan and smiles: "Sorry. Better forget you heard that"
Susan smiles her acquiescence.

THOMAS'S FLAT

Thomas comes in with two cups of tea. Jodie is sitting in Thomas's
chair. McLeary is on the floor beside her. Thomas puts her cup on the table
as gives a pit of cake to the dog and sips on his tea. McLeary licks Jodie's
foot as she takes her shoes off.

Thomas: "Do you always take your shoes off for interviews?" They
exchange a smile.

Jodie: "O Och, I don't know it's my first one. Do you think I should…?"

Thomas: "Well they are a wee wet. You know… I hadn't planned on
talking to anybody about it."

Jodie: "Well. It's not like I'm anybody you've known me since I was
a wee."

Jodie reaches into her bag and takes out a notebook and pen trying to
look professional barn."

Jodie: "Right. When are you planning to start?" Thomas: "Hold your
horses, lassie."

As Thomas cut another slice of cake and throw a slice to McLeary he
says:

"I may well have known you a while, but I don't want you turning
this into some kind of circus, for you and your newspaper. Just to sell
newspapers."

Jodie coughs: "We've already started an appeal for Hannah. I was up
at the hospital yesterday talking to Doctor Love. He told me if we can raise
enough money, they're to take Hannah to London to see the specialist.
Why did you get involved?"

Thomas get up and see an old milk carton, on the floor pick it up.

"Me? Oh. There's wee gang of them that come for the milk I've left over after my rounds and Hannah was one of them. I always thought of them as the family never had and when one goes missing, you feel responsible. I lost my family in the blitz so I know what it feels like."

Jodie: "That's why it's important that we get our message across. Now, will you please let me ask my questions?"

Thomas: "Och hell. Bossy. Just like your Mom. Alright, go ahead."

GLASGOW ROYAL

The Hospital Administrator's office, filing cabinets, big desk, papers, telephones, and a picture of the Administrator. Gloria, late 30's. with her husband and young daughter. She is talking on the phone. Doctor Love knocks and enters.

Gloria: "Well, sweetheart, Mummy's got to go now and I'll be home in a wee while." Gloria puts down the phone and smiles, before turning to Love.

Gloria: "Doctor Love… what can I do for you at this late hour?"

Love: "Gloria, it won't take a minute. These were handed in at reception…"

Love fans letters after letter like a running stream of money on Gloria's desk. Gloria: "did this benefactor have a name?"

Love: "No, he just came in and left them."

Gloria: "She's causing quite a stir our wee Hannah. I gather the Press is running an appeal."

Gloria looks at some of the amount.

Gloria: "They're going to need quite a bit more than this."

Love: "Yes, I know that, but this is a start. Can't we get the wheels in motion a bit faster?"

Gloria: "I've done all I can Michael. These things have a momentum of their own and neither heaven nor earth can move them along any quicker?"

Gloria sifts through the pile, as she does so she glances at her daughter's photo. Give a smile.

Gloria: "Let's see if I can't get them to bend the rules just this once."

Love: "Thanks, Gloria. You know I have a really funny feeling about this?" Gloria: "How's that?"

Love: "I truly believe they're going to make it."

CHAPTER 8

THE WALK

GLASGOW GRAND CENTRAL STATION

Centers on a collecting bucket, with a flyer being pasted onto it revealing a bucket is held in McLeary's teeth.

Thomas and crowd outside the station. A piper plays "Scotland the Brave". McLeary sits patiently with a collection bucket in his mouth. Thomas stands ready. He is wearing his tan shirt, with his S.A.S badges. Black Watch kilt and Glengarry badge and boots, a dirk tuck into his top sock, desert army boots circa 1941. He is carrying his rucksack.

The crowd is quite large: milkmen, from Thomas's depot, line the street with Union Jacks and Scottish's flags swaying in the light wind. Neighbors, hospital staff, doctor Jamieson, Stephen, John and Jodie, Sam, familiar faces from the Glasgow press office are all gathered around.

Thomas and McLeary are by two milk floats that are covered in banners and press cuttings relating to the appeal and the walk. Four nurses pass through the assembled crowd collecting money in buckets.

In the background, watching the proceedings from the inside of an old black Jaguar, sit Josh and Smokey. Both have cigarettes in their mouths and are watching the proceedings as Ian ducks through the crowd up to Thomas.

Josh: "There's that little shit McKeen. What's he up-to?"

As the two thugs watch closely, Ian reaches Thomas's side and urgently pulls at his shirt.

Ian: "Mr. McLeary, Mr McLeary."

Thomas: "Aye Ian, what is it? Can you not see I'm busy, man?"

Ian: "It's important. Those two guys that you saw off the other day, they're going to rob you along the way."

Thomas: "Ach, away with you Ian. Your imagination's playing tricks with you again." Ian: "No, no, I'm not lying. Honest. It's true. It's true."

Thomas: "Aye, aye, laddie. Now, away with you. Can you not see I've got to be on my way?" Thomas walks away from a disconsolate Ian. Jodie who has been watching, comes up to Ian.

Jodie:." Now then young Ian, what was so important that you wanted to tell Thomas."

Ian: "I'm scared for Mr McLeary. There are two guys after him. They're here and they're after stealing the money."

Jodie: "Ian McKeen. Stop it. Where do you get all these ideas from? Anyway, he'll be safe, we'll be watching his back".

Ian You're going with him?"

Jodie: "Aye. Me and John McLone - he's driving - That's his car over there." Ian: "Can I come with you ? Na tell the Lies."

Jodie: "Sorry, Ian. You've got school and you should be taking care of your Ma" Ian: "I wouldn't get in the way, honest."

Jodie: "I said, no. Now you just get yourself to the hospital and see Hannah and your Ma."

Ian walks disconsolately away, as Jodie joins John McLone. Jodie sidles up to Thomas.

Jodie: "Well. What a turnout, can you believe it Thomas?"

Thomas: "Aye, it's a scrum right enough! I did not expect so many, I'm choked... So much love she's a lucky girl, isn't she?"

Jodie: "She's lucky to have the likes of you about Thomas. That's the fact."

Thomas: "Aye, well... I can't wait to be off and neither can McLeary - he hates crowds."

GLASGOW ROYAL

Dr. Love is standing on the roof of the hospital with a pair of binoculars. He is looking at the crowd outside the station.

He homes in on Thomas. Thomas and McLeary begin their walk. Flanked by the two milk floats, a disorganized procession trails away from the station. Many people clap, approach and drop cash into the buckets cheering.

Love: "Good luck, my friend, we're going to need it, but time's against us, I'm afraid?"

In the Jaguar

Josh has a copy of the newspaper advertising the sponsored walk. He turns to Smokey.

Josh: "What did I tell you? It'll be a piece of cake. One old man and a shaggy bloody mutt."

Smokey: "I don't know. Doesn't feel right. He's doing it for that young kid in hospital."

Josh grabs Smokey's right ear and begins to twist it. Smokey's eyes water as he winces in pain.

Smokey (cont.): "OK. OK. Leave it out, you bastard. I didn't say I wouldn't help, did I?"

Josh: "You'd better not try and duck out of it, either. We need that money, more than some kid. It'll be your balls that'll be twisted if we don't get the money to repay Big Mac and it was you who lost the crack"

Smokey: "I wasn't to know the old Bill were watching me. I had to ditch it." Josh releases his ear and bangs. Smokey's head on the dashboard.

Josh: "If you hadn't been so stoned, you could have made a run for it. Anyways, no problem. Our friend over there's going to help us out. We'll just follow him for a few days and man, one night. Wham bam, thank you Man."

He slaps Smokey on the back, grins and drives off.

JOHN'S CAR/PETROL STATION

John is in the driver's seat. He takes a bite from a mars bar. Jodie is filling the tank.

John takes a pop at Jodie.

John: "You know she only takes five stars?"

Jodie rips the nozzle from the tank and shoves it back onto the pump which is labeled Five Star. Angrily, she goes to John' window and sticks her head in.

Jodie: "Okay! John. It's your choice. Let's get one thing straight. You know and I both know that this was my idea and so does Stephen and, before you say anything, I didn't tell him. As far as I'm concerned, you're the driver. It's my story. You've got the petty. I'm not paying for the petrol as well."

John pulls two fivers out of his wallet and gives them to her.

John: "Yes, miss and please could you get the chauffeur, a couple of sandwiches, a bar of chocolate and don't forget the Iron Brew while you're at it."

Jodie throws one of the notes onto his lap.

Jodie: "Fetch your own grub. I not surprised you've not got a girlfriend."
Jodie storms away towards the kiosk. As she goes.

John: "Touchy. Touchy. Let's see whether you're still so high and mighty after a few days on the road."

Jodie, angrily waves a hand in the air as she goes towards the cafe. John, reluctantly gets out of the car but not before he has thrown the half-eaten Mars Bar into the back.

HANNAS'S WARD. GLASGOW ROYAL.

It's night. Hannah is lying on the bed, still looking very ill. Mary is reading to her. The life support machinery is all working. Doctor Love enters.

"Doctor, I owe you an apology. I know you're doing the best you can, but the McKeen's have never charity cases.

Love: "No apologies needed and you shouldn't be thinking like that. There are times when we all need a little help from others"

Mary: "How so?"

Love: "This wee lass, has more support than we could ever have hoped for?" Love reaches and picks up Thomas's flyer from Hannas bedside table.

Inside the back of the car, the blanket covered with the flyers and a half-eaten Mars Bar – suddenly a hand reaches out and pulls the Mars Bar back under the blanket.

HANNAS'S WARD - GLASGOW ROYAL

Doctor love holds the flyer out to Mary.

Love: "He's just had a sendoff, you'd not believe. The newspaper appeal is already working, money's coming in all the time and I'm still pushing the administration."

Mary: "I can't believe it. Will there be enough time? And how's Jim doing and wee Ian? With all this going on, I've hardly had time to give them a thought."

Love: "Jim's doing fine and young Ian seems to be being looked after by the McFadden girl. You're a tough lot you McKeen's. Let's just pray that the money keeps on coming in?"

Mary: "Doctor, what do you think I've been doing every minute of the day." As Love leaves, Mary looks at Hannah and takes her hand.

Mary: "Hang on in, ma wee baby. Hang on."

JOHN MCLONES CAR

John, turns to Jodie.

John: "Jodie, I'm still hungry. Be a love and get that Mars bar I threw in the back just a while back."

Giving him a look, reluctantly, she turns in her seat and looks into the back - there are only the flyers, no Mars Bar.

Jodie: "There's no chocolate there.

John: "There must be." Look under the blanket."

Jodie turns round and getting on her knees on the front seat reaches over to pull the blanket back - she sees as she does her skirt rises up a little John can't help but look. Suddenly the care swerves: Ian, looking up at her.

John: "See it?"

Jodie: "You'd better pull over. We've got company." John: "What the hell do you mean?"

Jodie: "Just pull over, will you."

As McLone pulls into a lay-by, Jodie and Ian have a tug of war with the blanket.

Eventually, Jodie wins revealing Ian. The car comes to a halt and John sees Ian.

John: "Who the hell is he?"

Ian: "I'm Hannah's brother, Ian and I've got to warn Mr McLeary" John: "What about?"

Jodie: "He's got some cock and bull idea that Thomas is going to be robbed." Ian: "It's true! I told you. There's two guys…"

Jodie: "Now you just stop that, Ian McKeen. We've all had enough of your tall stories."

John: "Hold on Jodie. Give the lad a chance."

Jodie: "you keep out of this, John McLone. He's cried wolf too many times."

Ian: "No, really, honest. Mr McLeary saved me from a beating by two druggies. Then I heard them talking at the moto-cross. Said it would be a piece of cake."

John: "Listen, his Da' was shot by druggies. Druggies would kill their own mothers for money and there's been a lot of talk about this walk and the money. I can smell a good story, believe me".

She turns back and ignores them both. John turns and winks at Ian.

25 MILES FROM GLASGOW ROADSIDE. NIGHT 1

Thomas and McLeary are camped beside the road near a running stream the night is cool. A light wind moves, rustles through the trees outside a town. The camp is lit by street- light that over hangs from the road side. Thomas has set up a cooking pot on a stove on a trivet over a camp fire. The pot is steaming.

Thomas lean back on his bedding, writing in a journal. The next march thing, where to camp next. The map is lead out on the ground held by a couple of stones. Grounded next to Thomas's bedding roll between him and McLeary.

Thomas points to the map and talks to McLeary.

Thomas: "Well boy. We're here and we're going all the way down to there?" McLeary barks.

Thomas: "Yes, I know I'm hungry too. Let's see if it's ready." Thomas smells the pot.

Thomas: "Mmm. Smells good, boy."

In the pot is cooking some kind of meat stew. From his rucksack, he takes out two mess tins and looks at them. Thomas takes a breath, then beginning to ladle out the stew for each of them.

Thomas: "I haven't used these since forty-five. I knew they'd come in handy sometime"

He puts one on the ground in front of McLeary and pours a splash of water into it from an army issue water bottle. A small trickle of sand falls from the bottle into, McLeary's tin. Sorry about that, lad. Seems I brought a bit of the desert back with me. Thomas mutters.

ROADSIDE NIGHT - TWO TELEPHONE BOOTHS

Jodie is talking her mother about the day's events and John, unknown to Jodie talks to the editor.

Jodie: "Hi, Ma. It's me."

The sound of snoring -Jodie's dad in the back ground- is heard in.

Alice: "Jodie, how are you? I see… and you're where? How's it going. A pig is it? Well, just humor him, love. He can't be that bad, surely. Well, you're in my prayers darling… call again soon, won't you? Bye, no bye."

Alice puts down the phone and looks at her husband, smiling : he is still snoring in his chair.

Thomas is washing the mess tins in the stream. Jodie walks up carrying a half bottle of whiskey in one hand, Ian at her side.

McLeary barks a greeting. John stays in the background. Thomas: "Who's there?"

Jodie: "It's only me. I thought you might be in need of a night cap and I've brought a visitor!

From out of the shadows, Ian emerges into the light. Thomas, Shocked: "Well, where did you come from?"

Thomas looks at the bottle: "Good on you, young Jodie. There's a wee chill in the air, the night but what on earth is Ian doing here?"

Jodie: "He hid himself in the back of John's car before we left the station." Thomas: "What? I don't understand. Why?"

Jodie: "Ok Ian, tell Thomas what you told us."

Ian: "you remember the day you and McLeary sorted those two druggies out. Well I almost ran into them again, at the Motor Cross. They didn't see me and I overheard them planning to rob you."

Thomas: "Ian are you sure about this or is it another of yon fairy tales to get off school."

Ian; "Those guys were at the station watching you and I'm telling the truth. Honest! I know the car. It's a black Jar. On Hannah's life and she's my sister."

Ian has to fight back his tears. Thomas Looks at Jodie as if to say, what do you think.

Jodie: "Well, if he's telling the truth maybe he should come with us? He knows what car they're in and can keep his eyes open for them."

Ian: "Can I stay the night with you then, Mr. McLeary? I'll be nae bother." Thomas smiles: "No laddie, not the night, but sometime."

Ian smiles happily and bending down hugs McLeary. Lick his face. Jodie: "I'll get Stephen, my editor to let her know he's safe."

Thomas: "Which reminds me. I've been thinking. This is about Hannah. Your editor's, making money out of this, then he'd better give a thought to the paper contributing for Hanna? I reckon a couple of quid a mile good value."

Jodie take a wee nip: "Look, I'll be honest with you, I can't promise."

Thomas: "Well, you just go back" and talk to the big boss. Tell him, I've had another offer"

Jodie: "you haven't!"

Thomas smiles. Jodie gets up to go and pats McLeary on the head.

Jodie: "Ach. You're joshing me. Come on Ian. Let's get back to the hotel and get you to bed."

Jodie leads Ian away as Thomas gets his bedding roll and McLeary curls up beside him. Thomas looks up at the stars.

Thomas: "You know ladie they look the same where ever you are guiding our path." Not too far away behind the bushes, Josh and Smokey look at each other and grin. Smokey: "Okay, let's do it."

Josh: "Hold your horses. We're in nae hurry. He's going to get a lot more especially if that young McKeen's walking with him. More sympathy let's give him a couple more day and keep clear of the mutt."

booth.

THE ECHO PRESS OFFICE. DAY2

Stephen is in his office talking on the phone to Jodie. At a Post Office and at Phone

Stephen: "Ah. Jodie. How's it going?"

Jodie: "Fine… but we've acquired a fellow traveler. Hannah's brother, Ian.

Stephen: "Yes, I know, John told me? I think it'll give it the personal touch and if what he's saying about the druggies, we might have a real scoop? Listen Jodie. all's fair, and it's all for the good of the press."

Jodie: "And I'm still the little copy typist, right. Only good for making coffee."

Stephen: "No, no. John told me that the original story was your idea and this way we'd be getting two scoops in one. You're turning out to be a lucky paper girl, lassie. Now, what was it that Thomas wanted?"

Jodie: "Paper to donate a couple quid a mile"

Stephen: "Let make it fiver! Be an exclusive. I'll agree to that. The circulation's going up by leaps and bounds. Don't worry about John. Just remember he's a damn good reporter. Let's call it your learning curve! Okay? Tell Thomas he's got a deal"

He puts the phone down as does Jodie.

Jodie, to herself, counts: "I'll give him learning curve. He's got a few things to learn about Jodie McFadden He's never even thought about".

THE SCHOOL ROAD. DAY 2

Thomas and McLeary are passing a school by a crossroads Accompanied by a proud looking Ian, a new rucksack and bedroll on his back. Children line the fence and cheer him. And Thomas waves, smiling, faces wave back, Mc Leary give a couple of barks.

The sign on the crossroads says Manchester 281 miles.

JOHN'S CAR

John is eating while he drives, just finishing an egg and bacon sandwich. There is a dripping of egg on his shirt front and tie. Cigar is smolder in the ashtray, the car is filled with cigar smoke.

John, sarcastically: "Jodie, dearest…, could you pass me a tissue." Jodie balks, but remembers Stephen's words.

Jodie: "Where are they?" John: "In the glove box"

Jodie opens it and inside are tissues and a three-day old pork pie. Jodie takes out the pie between finger and thumb, disgusted.

Jodie: "What is this!?"

Jodie begins to wind down the window to throw it out. John: "I wondered where that dessert was? Hand it over." John grabs it and takes a bit. Jodie cannot believe her eyes.

John: "A little muster and that be Grand (Good)!"

John: "You've got a lot to learn, my girl. Eating on the job goes with the territory.

You've got to be prepared."

Jodie, sweetly: "Thank you John, but, when were you in the Boy Scouts? With Baden Powell? Watch out!"

Suddenly a black Jag being driven by Josh, dark glasses covering his face, races past them and at the last-minute swerves towards them, trying to force them off the road. John at the wheel, takes evasive action to avoid a collision. They come to a stop as the Jag speeds away.

Pulling in to a road sideway, John and Jodie get out and John inspects the car for damage.

John: "Well, at least there's no damage to my pride and joy."

Jodie: "Well, that's a relief! I don't suppose it crossed your mind to ask how I am?"

Jodie with a look of disgust at John gets back into the car and slams the door as John joins her and they drive off.

John: "Buckley up, be a dear"

THE A6 ROAD - EARLY EVENING

Outside Manchester, Thomas, McLeary and Ian are walking beside the road. Jodie and John pass in the car. They wave to each other.

Thomas: "Rather be with them in the lap of luxury?" Ian: "No ways. This an adventure for me."

Thomas: "Well, you just remember that we're doing it for no making' up fairy stories."

Ian: "You still don't believe me?"

At that moment, John draws up alongside them and Jodie gets out and runs to Ian. Jodie: "Thomas, we have just had a near miss by 2 guys driving a black jag"

Ian: "A black jag? Yes, that's Smokey and Josh!" John: "Now you believe I've a nose for a story?"

Thomas: "Who's he and what's that supposed to mean?" Jodie: "That's John McLone from the paper."

Thomas: "The one that's always giving you…" Jodie interrupts

Jodie: "Aye, but don't fash yourself about him."

She turns to Ian: "I think we owe you an apology, young Ian!"

Jodie: "I think that it's too dangerous for young Ian to stay with you?"

Thomas: "He who dares wins, not so Mr McLeary?"

Jodie: "What's that got to do with it? I still feel responsible for you and it's back to Glasgow for you, my lad."

Ian looks crestfallen. Thomas looks at the lad, then turns to Jodie.

Thomas: "Listen, Jodie, I know how to look after myself. God knows I've had enough practice. Ian will be with me during the day. They'll not try anything in broad daylight."

Jodie: "And at night, Thomas? I know you're a brave man but, I doubt you could handle two skellums in the dark on your own."

Thomas: "You're forgetting McLeary. He's the best security anyone could want. He'll give us fair warning and I've not forgotten my war-time training. It'd take more than two of them to do me any harm or young Ian here."

Ian: "Please, Miss McFadden. I can set booby traps and I am doing this for Hannah, you know?"

Jodie: "That's what worries me, I don't want your poor mother having more worries than she's got already."

She looks at the two of them, standing side by side. Thomas takes Ian's hand in his.

McLeary licks their hands. Jodie shrugs.

Jodie: "On two conditions. One you give John and I the money collected to put in the bank. Two you call into the office every morning and evening and, anything suspicious, you tell us. OK?"

Thomas nods his agreement, goes to his rucksack for the cash as Ian rushes forward to give Jodie a big hug. She looks down at him as tears well in her eyes. Hastily, she rejoins John in the car.

CHAPTER 9

WHAT'S ROUND THE CORNER

MRS ARGENT'S SHOP. EARLY MORNING, DAY 3

Mrs Argent is locking up the shop as Alice comes up. Mrs Argent is carrying a large bag.

Alice: "Finished for the day already, Mrs Argent? I was just coming to put something in kitty."

Mrs Argent: "Well, you can still do that. Being a bank Holiday, I'm closing up and away to see Mary".

Alice: "Would it be alright if I come with you? I haven't seen Mary in a while. I expect she could do with a chinwag."

Mrs Argent: "Aye. It can't be much fun with your barn in one ward and your hubbie in another. I'll be glad of the company. I've got a lot of money here, and with those skellums still on the loose, how do they say in the films, you can ride shotgun?"

The two women laugh as they walk to the bus stop.

CAMPSITE -STREAM - NORTH

Ian comes back into the camp carrying string and a small collection of tin cans. He empties the tin cans of stones as he enters. He then gets busy washing the tin plates, knives and forks from their breakfast. Thomas is packing the rucksacks and McLeary is on maid duty taking the plates to Ian who finishes them of.

Thomas: "By golly, young Ian, I'd rather feed you for a week than a fortnight.

Where'd you put it all?"

Ian: "I'm a growing lad, Mr. McLeary. Got to keep my strength up."
Thomas: "Aye. That's more than we had sometimes in the desert." Ian: "Adventure... Grand to see the world."

Thomas, Changes his voice: "Many never came back to tell about it." Ian: "What do you mean?"

Thomas: "Yes it was an adventure every day! You never knew what was around the corner. That was Lt Fadden motto. Fifty-four volunteers on our first raid to knock out German Messerschmitt in Egypt. There were twenty-five of us left to tell the tale. If it hadn't been for Jock Lewes and Captain Stirling that would've been the end of the SAS."

Ian looks amazed.

Ian: "Did you do any training?"

Thomas: "Aye lad, and tough it was too."

Thomas looks at his rucksack sawed in the Badge of the two wings.

Thomas starts to tell the story of the first time he met Lieutenant Jock Steele Lewes.

Thomas: "We were in the army camp, I was the oldest man in the group as we started the training".

ARMY CAMP - DAY.

Training officer, Jock Lewes, the S.A.S. is preparing for training.

A group of men in their late twenties desert combat gear. The man in the middle is Thomas.

An officer stands before them, over six-foot-tall, blond hair with diamond blue eyes and an iron jaw: lt is Jock Steel Lewes.

Behind them are a number of jeeps colored pink, incongruous against the green hills but it is the best camouflage color in the desert. Each jeep has a driver and their engines are running.

Jock gazes at the new recruits as he walks between them inspecting their kit.

Jock: "Good morning gentlemen. There is no ranking in this unit, you address me as Jock. I'm your trainer for today's exercise. Landing from a parachute drop. First, check that the packers have done their job. It's your life and once you're airborne, it'll be too late."

The recruits look at the parachutes at their feet. There are no planes around only the pink jeeps, engines idling.

"McLearey, you're with me"

The first four men grab the parachutes lying in front of them and mount the jeeps.

Jock grabs his and takes the last jeep as Thomas, parachute at the ready, sits next to him. The jeeps move away across the terrain. The convoy of jeeps come to a halt.

Thomas looks from side to side along the track. On either side of them makeshift runway deep trenches have been dug.

Jock, gets out of the jeep as the others draw to halt alongside.

Jock: "The jeeps will drive along this runway. When they reach twenty miles an hour, you will jump from the back and roll. There should be no hesitation. Remember, hesitation can get a man and his mates killed. Hesitate and you're out. Clear?"

The recruits look at each other, some determined, and others wary but in unison, salute and shout "Sir".

As the jeeps roll, Jock sits up right in the back with Thomas. On the other side sit two other men.

him.

The jeep speeds up the wheels faster, faster. Jock stands ready. Thomas looks up at

Jock grins: "OK. Your call McLearey"

Thomas, takes a quick look at the Speed'o on the jeep. As it reaches 20 mph, Thomas takes a deep breath then all four men jump out of the speeding jeep and roll to perfect landings Thomas brushes himself down then gazes at the other jeeps.

A couple of the other recruits from other jeeps are not so lucky. Some land wrong and Thomas sees some broken legs and arms.

Suddenly, Ian butts in a question: "But what were you supposed to be doing?"

Thomas: "The original aim was to try to find and destroy enemy aircraft on the ground in the western desert but this was broadened to deep road reconnaissance, logging all enemy movements and the third was to mount raids against the enemy's lines of communications. We would be parachuted into enemy lines"

Ian: "Sounds exciting. Bet you've got many more stories"?

Thomas: "Aye, that I have but, firstly there's work to do, have you forgotten? Now, pick yourself up and let's get on the road. We've a fair way to go yet"

Reluctantly, Ian dons his rucksack and with McLeary is in the lead. They head off south.

Days pass so do nights.

Encouragements. Many people and kids cheer them as they wend their way south.

People give them not only money but also food and cool drinks and, of course, water for McLeary.

IN THE MEAN TIME

Mrs Argent locks up the shop and head of with Alice towards the bus stop where they catch the bus to go to the hospital to visit Mary and see how young Hannah is doing.

Dr.Love, examines Hanna.

Smokey and Josh are drinking and playing pool in a local pub. Gloria is on the phone.

Jimmy and the Gang are out and about with tin cans for donations.

CAMPSITE 15

Thomas and Ian are preparing the camp. They are making a camp fire and they put the kettle on the fire which slowly comes to a boil.

Jodie comes up through the bushes followed by John, as McLeary runs up to them.

From high up in a tree, Josh sits watching and waiting.

Thomas: "Oh. Hi there, Jodie. How are you?"

Jodie. "Not so bad. Police still looking for that two"

Josh hears what Jodie says. Jumping down from his hiding place in the tree, he makes a runner for it towards where Smokey is.

Josh, underneath his breath, thinking of Thomas: "Your days are numbered"

Thomas." Aye. Glad to have the company of young Ian here, even if he does 'nae stop prattling on all day or eating. Fair gives me a thirst."

Ian: "How's Me Ma, Pa and Hannah fairing, Miss McFadden?"

Jodie: "Your Da's fine, up and about already, but your Ma's fair going out of her head worrying about Hannah."

Thomas, She not so hot, then Jodie?"

Jodie: "Doctor Love thinks she's holding her own but time is running out."

John steps out of the shadows and approaches the group. McLeary gets up and stands by Thomas and growls. John steps sharply backwards.

Jodie introduces him again: "Oh, I'm sorry, Thomas, as I mentioned before, this is John McLone, also from the paper. I told you about him"

Thomas: "Aye, that you did Jodie. From the way he came skulking in, I'm thinking you'd better watch yourself. Your ideas will not be the only thing he'll have off your back, if you're not careful."

John: "That's a bit hard, Thomas"

Thomas: "The name's Mr. McLearey to you."

John: "Look. I'm sorry if we seem to have got off on the wrong foot. I'm only here to help Jodie"

Jodie: "You could've fooled me. Not content with stealing my ideas, you've tried to treat me like a skivvy since we left Glasgow"

John: "I'm an old hand and maybe I do rub peoples back up the wrong way but this job makes you very cynical"

Thomas: "Listen. I was in the S.A.S from the beginning. You know how many volunteers there were to join. Seven hundred and only twelve passed the criteria. Just be thankfull"

John, a little take back: " I'm sure you're right, Thomas...Mr McLearey, but, that doesn't take away from the fact that those skellums are after you and the monies. And I'm more interested in this story".

Jodie: "And making sure you look after young Ian" Thomas: "Fine, John! And the name's Thomas." The two men shake hands in an uneasy truce.

Jodie: "Well, I'm glad that's settled but we're here for another story for my column. My editor loved that wee story you told me about Mrs. McGinty and the sheep getting drunk on the apple wind fall."

Thomas: "Aye - true enough - pure cider it was. I thought that might tickle your reader's fancy. Would you all like a cup of tea. Can'nae vouch for what it's like, young Ian made it".

As Ian pours the four cups of tea.

Thomas: "Ian. You've drunk enough to sink a battle ship" As Jodie and John hide their smiles,

Thomas: "My boy, make the best of it while you can. So you're here for the next installment, but I can't promise you it's got anything to do with sheep getting drunk"

Ian: "Tell them about Jugular Jim?

Jodie: "Sounds promising. So, Thomas, who was this Jugular Jim?" Thomas: "It was the winter. Cold! Boy was it, as I recall…"

Jodie takes out her notebook and starts writing. John lays back and relaxes lighting a cigar. Ian sits beside McLearey, stroking him.

Josh disappears back to Smokey.

Thomas: "I'd just started my training and got my strips. My commanding officer came up and asked if I'd like to do special combat training for a new squad".

John: "Thomas, excuse me, when was this?" Thomas: "Just listen boy"

John glances at Jodie. Jodie grins.

OLD RUN DOWN AERODROME -1941

1941. I was sent to join a new unit known as Z force, up in a secret base near Fort William in Scotland, a snowy Mounties' wet ass of a places. I was made Team Leader.

There were sixteen members to each team. A DC 7 like a large silver bird was rousting in an old air hangar where we trained

There were different groups of sixteen young men standing around in combat gear. Some were wearing dark red berets. The dark red berets let other soldiers know they were the Paras from 21st Division. Other guys had green one from the Royal Engineers. Most of the men were smoking.

I was a Para! We were chatting, away to each other.

Suddenly, there was a roar from the back of the hangar as a large man marches over towards us. We soon found out he was named Jugular Jim. He said:

- Put those cigarettes out before you burn the place down. This isn't the public bar". He snapped.

Suddenly, he pulled a machine gun from behind his back and began to fire. All the volunteers dived for cover until the firing had stopped. No-one moved.

Standing before us was a big brute of a man over six foot tall. Black bearded. Hands like sledgehammers. He was wearing the same combat gear as us but he had a Gray beret on.

He grinned at us, like a Cheshire cat that had got the mouse and the cream and said:

- Those of you who are still alive and have not shit your pants, on your feet!

Slowly, all but two of the group got to their feet. Two soldiers remained on the ground.

- That, gentlemen was an exercise in expecting the unexpected I checked out the two and I was angry!
- Sir. Permission to speak! Jugular Jim gave me a grim smile and nodded
- Shouldn't we look after the dead men and you had no right to shoot a fellow soldier in cold blood, sir
- Is that so laddie? I'll be sure to remember your name when I get to write my report. At least one of you got balls to face me off. O.K. lads, on your feet now."

To our amazement, the two "dead" soldiers got to their feet smiling and saluted Jugular Jim who said:

- The blood you see, gentlemen, is known in the film industry as Kensington Gore. Very life like, do you not think? If that had been live ammo, you'd all be dead and your mothers would be greeting over those little soggy, black edged telegrams. Now, we wouldn't want that, would we? My name is James Macpherson. I'm here to prevent that. It is quite simply, gentlemen, the art of sending your enemy to Hades.

Jim stepped forward and almost as one, the men took a step back. He raised his chin and there was a white line across his throat where the hair had refused to grow back.

- You will notice an irregularity in my bearded which is where a man imagined that he could sever my jugular. I was not un-expecting the unexpected which is why I am here, as living proof of that. I am known as Jugular Jim and there's many a man has come to regret upsetting me. Now, there are many ways of killing a man.

BACK TO CAMPSITE

John and Jodie's eyes light up. John, coughs on his cigar.
Thomas: "Are you alright there, John".
Thomas winks and smiles at Jodie.
John: "No. No. I'm fine. A little cold maybe. A shot of your whisky wouldn't come amiss though".
Thomas grins and hands him a hip flask with the S.A.S badge engraved and the motto "WHO DARE WIN".
Ian: "Did you ever have to kill a man with your bare hands, Mr.McLearey?" Thomas looks around him - he sighs deeply

Thomas: "I'm no proud of it young Ian, but, it was kill or be killed at that time and there was only a war widows's pension for getting yourself killed. I pray you'll never have to see those times again laddie"

John': "Amen to that!

Jodie: "Have the true beginnings of the S.A.S, ever been recorded?"

Thomas: "Aye, they have. I've got the book here with me in it. Takes me back to the good times I had with McLearey's grandpa but it also reminds me of the pain at losing so many mates. I'm a wee bit tired now, so, you'll forgive me if I bid you good night. Ian and I have got to be up with the lark tomorrow, if we're to meet our schedule. Doubtless, we'll see you on the morrow?"

Jodie and John make their good buys and leave. Thomas, and Ian set to arranging their beds and Ian throws. McLeary a biscuit.

As Jodie and John walk away, Thomas falls back and gazes up at the stars.

EXT CAMPSITE AND JAGUAR

Night sky.

Josh approaches the Jaguar. Smokey asleep. Silently, Josh carefully opens the car door and wakes Smokey with a hit to his stomach.

Smokey: "What the hell? I was only having a kip, you told me to watch over the car?"

Josh;" Suppose you could do that with your eyes shut you eejit.' I could hear your snoring back at the old man's camp"

Smokey: "You hear anything interesting?"

Josh: "Aye! We've got our work cut out they know we're after them".

Smokey" How?"

Josh: "When you tried to run them off the road, that little snitch McKeen had seen us at Glasgow Central and told them what car we had."

Smokey: "He'll get a right pasting when I catch up with him. Anything else?"

Josh: "I know but they made us and there is more. Just some guff about when he was in the army. Nothing to worry us".

Smokey: "What about the bloody dog?"

Josh smiles and pulls a gun from his coat pocket. Josh: "That'll be nae problem with this"

Smokey look alarmed.

Smokey: "Where'd you get that for Christ's sake? I'll not be wanting to be up in front of the beak on a count of murder."

Josh: "Don't wet yourself. You canna be done for shooting a dog in self-deafens. Besides, we'll be long gone. He should have a fair wee bit in that rucksack of his by now. Enough to sort The Big 'Yun out and still make a good score."

CHAPTER 10

THE JAM JAR

CHILDREN'S WARD. GLASGOW ROYAL. NIGHT.

A large black Charge Nurse sits at her desk sipping a cup of tea. Her name plate reads Dudu Mtota. On Nurse Mtota's lap is latest edition of Jodie's newspaper. Mary is asleep in the corner with a blanket around her. There is a sudden sound from outside the room, Nurse Mtota puts her tea down and leaves the room to investigate.

HANNAS'S ROOM DOOR

An old jam jar appears held by young Jimmy, dirty face, untidy hair and wearing an old shirt and blue shorts. He climbs in through the window. Very carefully, he places the jam jar, full of tanners by Hannah's door.

Jimmy climbs out of the open window and down to where the little gang wait for him. Nurse Mtota, returns to Hannah's and, as she sits herself down she hears a sneeze from outside the window. On the hallway to Hanna room, she opens the window, peers out to see eight children crouching down in the dark. Jimmy wipes his nose with a dirty handkerchief and smiles along with the other children. Jimmy gets nudge from one of the other children. He looks up. Nurse Mtota is looking down at them.

Jimmy: "Please, miss, how's our Hannah doing? We all miss her and want her back" Nurse Mtota: "She's doing fine. Now be off with you. It's long past your bedtime"

As Nurse Mtota looks out of window, she smiles. All you can see it those white teeth.

She closes the window.

"I'll give this to Gloria in the morning" Mtota murmurs to herself. "All her mates – Love". Nurse Mtota smiles then gazes Hannah and places the jam jar on the table next to the bed and moves back out of the room as quite as a mouse.

JODIE'S HOTEL ROOM. NIGHT

Jodie is at her typewriter.

Her clothes are all over the place. Pink bras are draping off a chair and other woman's stuff with Jodie's notepad lie on the dressing table with a square mirror. Phone rings.

Jodie: "Stephen. You'll never guess who this Thomas McLeary is?" Stephen (Voice): "I hope it's going to sell the story"

Jodie: "I don't think you'll be sorry?"

Stephen (Voice): "Okay. Get on with it. I'm paying for the call" Jodie: "He was a Founder member of the SAS with a Jock Lewes"

Stephen: "Yes and Captain Stirling, if my memory serves me right? That should help circulation. Get all you can on him and I'll check him out this end".

Jodie. (Indignant): "I don't think he's lying?"

Stephen: "I'm not saying he is, but, the more background we can get, the better the story"

Jodie: "Sorry, you're right. I'm sure this is really going to make the readers go for our guy. Thomas was in one of the first SAS units in Africa. Oh, I told him about the donation. We've got the exclusive…"

Stephen: "I told you you're our lucky omen" There is a knock at Jodie 'a door.

Jodie: "Stephen can I call you back?… Right… Bye now"…

Jodie goes and opens the door. John is standing there with a bottle of champagne and two glasses. He marches in and plunks himself on the bed, puts the bottle and glasses on the side table. He has already had a few drinks. Jodie watches him, her jaw dropping.

Jodie: "What the hell do you think you're doing?"

John: "Credit where credit's due, you've got a great story coming out here and I thought a little celebration might be in order?"

John notices the bra at the notebook and grins.

Jodie: "Oh, you did, did you? You just hold your horses"

Jodie picks up the champagne and glasses and thrusts them back into John's hands.

Jodie (Cont.): "If you think a couple of hours under the stars is going to buy you a ticket into my pants. You've got another think coming. Come on!"

Jodie pulls him to his feet by his lapels.

Jodie (Cont.): "You have no bloody idea, do you?" Jodie frog marches him out…

Jodie: "You are one of the most disgusting human beings on this earth. I wouldn't pass a second of my time in the same country as you, let alone a room, if we weren't stuck with each other on this assignment. Understand? Now out!"

Jodie ejects John into the corridor and slams the door. John: "I think she likes me?"

John falls over in the hotel's corridor, saving the champagne, as two guests walk by. Jodie turns and leans back against the door exasperated. She slides down into a sitting position against the door, and shakes her head in despair. Jodie (to herself):

"If anyone deserves champagne, it's Thomas"

OUTSKIRTS OF BIRMINGHAM

Thomas and McLeary are walking past a signpost "Birmingham" John is driving. Jodie sits, tightlipped beside him.

John: "Look, I'm sorry about last night. I'd had a couple of drinks and thought ..."

Jodie: "That's just your problem John. You don't think, or if you do, it's through your backside. Now shut it. Let me concentrate on looking out for that black Jag.

ROYAL HANNA

Hannas' nurse Mtota leads Mary through into the ward which is now bedecked with cards and flowers. Nurse Mtota points to the bed where Hannah still lies, connected to various machines. There, on the bed side table is the jam jar full of six pences. She reads the note and sits down next to Hannah. Tears well up in her eyes.

Nurse Mtota: "She may not know it now, but, she's a lucky girl to have so many friends and so much love."

Mary smiles through her tears and nods holding Hannah' hand.

CAMPSITE

Thomas, Ian and McLeary are preparing for a good night's rest. The bedrolls are laid out and Thomas has just lit the primus stove. Through a narrow track leading to the site, the black Jag cautiously makes its way. The car comes to a stop and Josh and Smokey get silently out, being careful to close the doors as quietly as possible.

Thomas is busy reading the Lewes book by the light of his flash lamp, lying by primus stove. McLeary has his eyes shut but his ears, which twitch now and then, show evidence that he is still alert. Ian is setting out his booby traps around the immediate perimeter of their sleeping area.

JOHN'S CAR

Jodie sits silently, clutching the bottle of whiskey as John drives along. John (smiles): "One day you'll believe me"

The car draws into the track leading to the camp. John (cont.): "Hello? What's this? Visitors?"

The track is blocked by the Jag. They come to a stop

Jodie: "That's the car that tried to cut us up the other day"

John: "I don't like the look of this. Our skellums have returned. You stay here, I'll go investigate"

Jodie: "Not on your life John McLone. I'm coming with you"

Together, they get out of the car, walk up to the Jag looking inside. Seeing nothing, they creep forward.

Josh and Smokey cautiously approach the campsite. Josh has the gun in his hand. He stops and points. Through the bushes, they can see Ian setting his traps.

Josh whispers: "There's that little toe rag, McKeen. Think you can handle him on your own, but quiet? Don't want to warn that fecking dog"

Smokey smiles and takes a cosh from his back-pocket Smokey: "Nae bother"

Josh (nods): "Fine. Then get him into the boot of the car" Smokey: "Why?"

Josh: "He's our "Get out of Jail" free card".

Smokey creeps around behind Ian and, as he turns to go back to the camp, Smokey knocks him unconscious and putting him over his shoulder carries him back to the Jag.

John and Jodie hear the noise of Smokey carrying Ian to the car. They watch as the unconscious boy is bundled into the boot of the car. Jodie is about to leap out when John holds her back. She is furious.

John (whispers): "Patience, my girl. Let them think they've got an ace in the hole" When Smokey is clear, John and Jodie run to the Jag open the boot and get Ian out.

As he is coming to, John has to hold his mouth shut to stop him yelling out a warning.

John: "Quiet laddie. You'll get your chance"

Ian looks round and sees Jodie, who takes his hand and smiles at him. He shrugs and rubs the back of his head.

CAMPSITE

Smokey rejoins Josh and gives him the thumbs up. Josh nods and whispers.

Josh: "you get around the other side and whistle. The olden's bound to send the dog to investigate"

Smokey looks at Josh in amazement.

Smokey: "Up your jacksie. And then what the feck am I going to do?"

Josh (smiling): "Probably shit yourself? Get up a tree, you dipstick where the dog canna' reach you. The old man calls for the dog when he sees me and I'll threaten to shoot the dog unless he hands over the dosh. Easy, peaz!"

Smokey is none too happy about the plan.

Smokey: "It might be for you - you've got the gun."

Josh: "Quit blathering and get going. Whistle me when you're up the tree and remember, we've still got the toe rag"

Smokey disappears into the bushes;

Josh wait impatiently, gun in hand. Thomas is still reading. McLeary suddenly opens his eyes and growls softly.

Thomas: "What is it McLeary? Someone about?"

Suddenly, there is a whistle from the other side of the camp. McLeary looks at Thomas.

Thomas, (cont.): "Aye, lad - go see, I'll be fine"

As McLeary lopes off into the darkness, Thomas is halfway to standing upright when Josh appears holding his gun.

Thomas: "What the hell do you want, you skellum?"

Josh: "Now, now, old yun - that's no way to greet a fellow Glaswegian and you're in no position to be calling me names. Where's the money?"

Thomas: "Oh, so it's money you're after is it? Well you're in for a wee surprise, m'boyo. You'd not be daft enough to think I'd be carrying all that cash around?"

Josh: "You're lying old 'Yun. It's Bank Holiday, you've not been near a bank. We've been watching you."

Thomas: "Then, no doubt, you've seen I've security. MacLarey! As MacLarey emerges at a run from the bushes, Josh raises his gun and points it at the oncoming dog."

Josh: "You'd better stop him there or he's dead meat" Thomas cannot risk his dog's life.

He shouts: "McLeary! Stay - Down – Stay"

TRACK TO CAMPSITE

As McLeary lies down, Thomas's voice reaches John and Jodie. They stop. They look at each other. John nods to Ian to get up into a tree and wait. As they creep nearer to the campsite, through the bushes, they see Thomas standing upright, his feet straddling the rucksack, McLeary sitting, poised, and waiting for an opportunity to spring, Josh with his gun and Smokey, as he appears from the bushes.

Thomas: "What a brave lad - reinforcements!" Smokey: "Has he got the money?"

Thomas: "Aye lad! It's between my legs. You man enough to come and get it?" Smokey looks helplessly at Josh.

CAMPSITE PERIMETER, BUSHES

Jodie looks at John - what to do - John nods for her to give him the bottle of whiskey

- questioningly she does so. John takes his coat off and tears a sleeve off his shirt. Opening the whiskey, he pours some of it onto the material, take a quick dram. Pushes it into neck of the bottle.

He motions for Jodie, to duck and taking his lighter out sets light to the shirt sleeve. When it is a light, he throws it at the primus stove which erupts. There is a massive explosion as the whiskey goes up in flames. McLeary takes the opportunity to jump at Josh knocking the gun out of his hand which lands on the ground just out of reach of Thomas.

Smokey, seeing the game is up starts running away through the trees and right into a flying kick from Ian in the trees almost knocking him out but as he does so, Ian, himself, falls, and is winded. Smokey sees an opportunity grabs him round the neck and pulls him along through the trees to the jag.

Thomas looks around him. McLeary is standing guard over Josh. At the sound of Ian's shouts, he momentarily takes his eyes of Josh who makes a dash for the gun and aims it at the snarling McLeary. Jodie, John and Thomas look around the campsite helplessly, as Josh backs off through the bushes.

Thomas (shrugs): "That was an awful waste of good whiskey John, but thanks"

Jodie, a little impressed: "We'd better get to the nearest phone box, ring the police and give them the description of the two skellums, the car they're driving and warn them that they're armed"

ROADSIDE NEAR BRISTOL. MORNING 9.

Thomas and McLeary have just struck camp. Thomas swings his rucksack onto his back and heads off, seemingly not the worse for wear for the coming night events. And the excitement last night.

DOCTOR JAMIESON'S SURGERY

Dr Jamieson is just seeing a patient out when his receptionist brings him a large brown envelope.

Jamieson: "What've you got there, Myra?"

Receptionist: "The results of the tests you wanted done on Thomas McLeary"

Jamieson: "Oh, aye. There's a wee problem but I need to talk to him about. Just put them on the desk. I'm just off to see Mrs Cameron. She'd have me there twenty-four hours a day, if she could."

The receptionist, smiling, puts the envelope on the desk.

BRISTOL HOTEL ROOM

Jodie sighs while she is typing up her story. There is a knock at the door. Jodie gets up and answers it. John is standing there with two glasses and another bottle of, looking hopeful. Jodie shakes her head.

John: "I'd have thought that a little drink might help"

Jodie: "John, you were great last night and I've given you a great write up, but, sadly, you're still a long way off my idea of being a knight in shining armour... Sorry?"

John: "You have a safe night Jodie." Jodie grins and shakes her head.

Jodie: "Don't worry. When the girls read my story, they'll be crawling all over you.

You'd better go see if you can get a refund on that."

She smiles and closes the door, leaving a forlorn John walking away down the corridor.

GLASGOW CENTRAL - DR LOVE'S OFFICE

Dr Love is studying some X-Rays on a light box when his phone rings. He goes and picks it up.

"Jamieson s' surgery"

Love: "Love here. Oh, hullo, Jamie. What's to do?"

Jamieson: "Never rains but it pours, Thomas has an aneurysm" Love: "What type?"

Jamieson: "Aortic abdominal. He's going to need an angiography as soon as possible"

Love: "Aye. You're right. The last thing he should be doing is carrying a rucksack and living wild. Leave it with me, Jamie, I'll see if I can locate them?"

Jamieson: "How's young Hannah?"

Love: "As well as can be expected. She's stable, but time's not on our side and Gloria's fighting like a dervish to unravel the bureaucracy. We'll speak later"

Dr. Love puts the phone down and then picks it up again and asks the telephones to get him the editor of The Echo

THE ECHO - EDITOR'S OFFICE.

Stephen is giving some dictation to a secretary when the phone goes. The secretary picks it up and hands it to Stephen.

"It's for you, Doctor Love from the Royal"

Stephen (cheerful): "Hello, Doctor. Happy with the campaign and young Judie's' dailies on Thomas and the SAS?"

Love: "Yes, they're doing wonders for the campaign! Unfortunately, they're going to have to stop?"

Stephen: "Why in God's name?"

Love: "Thomas has an aortic abdominal aneurism. It could burst at any time. Carrying that load is the last thing he should be doing. Can you contact them?"

Stephen: "I'll try but they're on the road, Jodie calls me in her story every night. I'll try the hotel where they were last night.

Hold on… He picks up another phone.

ROAD TO EXETER/ JAG.

Josh is driving. Beside him Smokey sits watching the road. Ian is tied up in the back on the floor. Smokey suddenly turns to Josh.

Smokey: "Are you feckin' mad this road leads down to Lands'End. That's where that Auld git's going"

Josh: "That's exactly why I'm going that way. Mr. Plod and his mates will think that we'll be heading north and they'll be on the lookout. They won't be looking around here!"

Smokey: "Where are we going to stay? We can hardly book into a hotel with him trussed up like a turkey?"

Josh: "Whilst you and his nibs back there were in the land of nod, I phoned the Big'Yun. Remember when he was smuggling the crack in down here? He's still got an old barn near a mine; we can keep in just near Lands' End. Let's ransom the kid for the money we were going to nick. I'll negotiate from there. They'll concentrate their thoughts up there, back in Glasgow"

Smoky: "That's brilliant"

Josh: "That's why you're with me! I've got the…"

CHAPTER 11

THE URGENT MESSAGE

EDITOR'S OFFICE

Stephen is getting angry on the phone. He slams the phone down and picks the other one up.

Stephen: "Sorry, Doctor. No luck. They checked out this morning and didn't say where their next stop was going to be"

Love: "I just hope we're not too late. When, and note, I say when and not if the aneurism bursts, it'll be too late"

Stephen: "As soon as I can, I'll contact you. Bye"

He replaces the phone with a worried sigh and speaks to himself. Stephen (between his teeth): "Come on Jodie, call me, please?"

THE EXETER ROAD. LATE DAY

Thomas and McLeary stop walking.

Thomas: "I hope the Laddie Ian is OK? We are on the home stretch, boy" McLeary barks. Puts down his rucksack. Signpost. "Exeter".

As they start to make camp Thomas notices the head lights of a car. It is John and Jodie. They walk over to Thomas who is just getting the food ready for McLeary and himself.

John: "That Jugular Jim story captured the imagination of the public. We checked it out"

Thomas looks up angrily

Jodie: "Hold on Thomas. We've all been working so hard on this whole story and successfully, our competition would like nothing better than to get people to think that this was all just some cheap publicity stunt to sell our newspaper."

Thomas: "I've thought you'd be better employed trying to find young Ian. I fear for him. I told you I did nae want this to become a circus"

Jodie: "We've had his picture printed on the front page of the Echo and other papers and TV have picked it up as well. In order to keep the momentum going and the public interested, have you any other stories?"

Thomas (grins): "Oh aye, many times but, also with another brave man just like our Laddie Ian"

Thomas looks, up at the night sky a crest moon.

DESERT NORTH AFICA S.A.S CAMP NIGHT.

Thomas: "Men who volunteered were of a different ilk to your average soldier. Madcap Paddy Blair Mayne was the most decorated soldier in the war. Irish, with a rogue streak, the top brass could'nae fathom.

Our assignment was to wipe out a group of top German brass in a house. The intelligence your father that I rescued, got from that German

Officer gave us all the info. What he brought back had told us that they were there to co-ordinate a series of air raids.

In addition, our target was to destroy the bombers that had just flown in from Sicily. Madcap Paddy, I and eight other men crept down to the fence and dug, like foxes into a chicken coup, underneath the wire. It was all quiet, just a searchlight passing from time to time. We came in on the south side.

All the bombers were lined up like a mass of gray death ready to bomb their targets on the north. There was a Luftwaffe control tower and a petrol tanker and a huge pile of ammo,

CAMPSITE

Jodie and John are dumbstruck by the nonchalance with which Thomas has told his tale. Jodie is the first to break the silence.

Jodie: "So it was you who saved my Da's life?"

Thomas: "Aye, but we agreed to keep it secret. Can I get back? Anyways, Paddy was a rugby player, played for Ireland. You should have seen him move, like a gazelle. The rest of the lads made it inside.

Thanks to the plans, we knew where the planes would be and more important, we knew that fighters and loaded bombers would be mixed together: big mistake!

So, once we were inside of the compound of the Luftwaffe, I gave the orders to split into two different groups of 6.

The first group were to take out the bombers and the fighter planes by explosive devices that would be attached to the fuselage of some of the bombers, knowing that the explosion of the bombers would set off a domino effect.

The explosive devices would be on a 15 minutes time fuse and the rest of us, the other group of 6 would concentrate on taking out the control tower and the ammo dump as quickly and quietly as we could!

97

15 minutes later, all hell broke loose. The planes exploded one by one! We ceased the control tower and we took out the men inside. All at once, the ammo dump exploded.

There was rapid gun fire from both sides as we made our escape. We lost a few good men on that day!

John: "How many planes were demolished?"

Thomas: "According to intelligence, about 280. What was more important, we stopped the devastation and took the Lufthansa by surprise and we destroyed their moral"

Jodie: "Did you get a medal?"

Thomas: "Aye lassie, the Military Cross and McLeary's grandpa got the canine equivalent."

Jodie hugs McLeary.

Jodie: "Your Grandpa' saved my Da's life! That'll be something to tell Stephen" John: "It'll have to wait until tomorrow Jodie: It's too late for tomorrow's edition." Jodie looks at her watch and nods sadly.

THE ECHO - EDITORS' OFFICE - EVENING.

Stephen. Is in his office working at his desk. The phone rings.

Stephen: "Hi Jodie! Sorry, Jim… McLean… oh I see, is that right? So he was eh? O.K., that's all I need. Great news. I owe you a large one next time I see you"

Stephen replaces the handset and picks up another phone. Stephen: "Okay, Mac. Let the presses roll"

Headline as follows:

"Hannah's Angel of Mercy is S.A.S. Hero!"

And underneath the photo of Smokey, Josh and young Ian:

"This boy, brother of Hannah, has been kidnapped by these 2 men. Please call the police or the Echo if you see them. All calls will be anonymous"

As he replaces the phone, he murmurs to himself.

"Come on Jodie, ring, for God's sake, otherwise he'll be a dead hero!"

Stephen puts down the phone and takes a bottle of scotch from drawer and pours a glass. The phone goes again. Eagerly, he picks it up.

Stephen: "Jodie, Thank God! Oh, it's you Doctor. No, sorry, I can't understand it. It's not like her to miss a deadline" He nods.

Stephen: "Of course, you'll be the first to know"

HANNAS'S WARD

Nurse Myota is changing one of Hanna's drips. Mary is standing by. They exchange grim glances.

Mary: "I don't know what the world's coming to, nurse. First, Hannah, now Ian and the news about Thomas"

Nurse Mtota: "Aye, Doctor Love's fair sweating blood. You wouldn't think it would be so difficult to find a soul these days"

DISUSED TIN MINE NIGHT

The Jag draws up outside the unused offices of a disused tin mine. In the background can be seen the skeleton of the tin mine elevator stack. Smokey roughly pulls Ian out from the back of the car and frog marches him into the building.

Josh carries some bags of food in and tries the cooker which lights up. The room is sparsely furnished. A table, three chairs and, in the corner an old sofa

Josh: "This much better than a barn, we even got gas. OK, Smokey make yourself useful. Get cooking. It's a good job I thought to buy enough food to last us out."

Ian: "I need to go for a shit'

Smokey: "Shit in your pants." But he looks over to Josh for agreement. Josh nods. Smokey goes over to him and unties the ropes around his wrists.

Smokey: "OK, but you try and run off and you'll no walk again"

He brandishes the gun at Ian's kneecaps. Ian nods his understanding.

ADMINISTRATION OFFICE

Gloria is on the phone and Love sits opposite her, very nervous. She is obviously angry.

Gloria: "No! You just listen to me for once. Our Charity Campaign has raised almost half of the necessary funds. The least you can do is match it minister"

She listens to an anonymous voice at the other end.

"That's bull. If you don't like my tone, tough. No action and I'm going to make sure the press name you and shame you...Don't threaten me with libel" she barks. "There isn't a judge in the land who will have any sympathy with your office, not only now but never"

She slams the phone down and looks across at Love who's silently clapping his hands.

Love: "Gloria, that was great, thank you. Now, if only we could find that damned man, his dog and now the boy"

Gloria: "Ever think of local radio? Someone's bound to hear it and get in touch?"

Love rushes out of the office, calling out over his shoulder.

Love: "You are brilliant. I'll phone McLean at The Echo, he'll have some contacts?"

MCLONES' CAR - TRAVELLING DAY

The car radio is playing some pop music of the time Jodie is busy making notes for her next report to Stephen. She begins to read

Jodie: "What do you think of this?"

McLone leans forward to switch channels on the car radio. McLone: "Crap!"

Jodie: "Thanks very much"

McLone: "Not your … the music…Oh! Listen up!" Jodie and McLone listen intently to the broadcast.

Radio Announcer's voice: "We are interrupting this broadcast to appeal to all travelers in the South Devon, Cornwall area. Please be on the lookout for a man, Thomas McLeary and his Alsatian dog.

It is imperative that anyone seeing them contact the police immediately. Mr. McLeary has a serious condition which requires urgent hospital treatment. Also, please keep your eyes open for a black Jag car which may be travelling north. It contains two young men who have abducted a young boy. The public are warned not to approach the men who are armed"

McLone pulls the car over to the side of the road and looks at Jodie. Jodie: "What do you think the problem is?"

"No idea, but, it's funny there's no mention of Hannah?"

Jodie: "Positively thinking hopefully means that she's not the prime concern. But how in hells' name do we find them? Knowing Thomas, he'll be trolling the villages."

John sees a phone box in the distance.

"I'll go phone the police and Stephen. Let them know where we are and alert the local bobbies"

GLASGOW ROYAL HANNAH'S ROOM. EVENING.

Doctor Love and two nurses are preparing Hanna for the journey and checking all the machines. Mary is holding Hanna's hand. Hanna is still very ill. The door opens and two porters enter with specially adapted trolley.

Love: "She's fine. Pulse is strong. It's going to be alright and it's just the tonic your husband needs as well."

Nurses finish with the machinery and nod to Love.

Mary: "I've prayed for this moment every minute of every day! It'll give Jim a lift as well?"

ROADSIDE FROM DAY 12.

Jodie watches anxiously as John approaches the car.

John: "We're in luck. They're not far from here. Been spotted just outside Penances." Jodie: "But why the radio message and what's the news on Hannah?"

John: "Good news and bad. Hannah's going to be OK. She's on her way to London but it's Thomas. He's got an aneurism which needs urgent treatment otherwise, he'll not see Lands-End"

John jumps into the car and they speed away.

CORNISH BORDER

Thomas and McLeary are approaching a sign "Duchy of Cornwall"

John and Jodie come to a screeching halt. Beside them is a Jaguar police car, out of which jump a couple of local policemen and a doctor carrying a bag.

Thomas: "What's all this about? We dinn'ae want a police escort. Have you found Ian?" Jodie jumps out of the car and rushes to Thomas. John stays in the car.

Jodie: "Thomas. Hannah's going to be OK. They're moving her to London today" Jodie gives Thomas a huge hug. McLeary barks and chases his tail.

Thomas: "God be praised! But why the police escort! God forbid it's for Ian?" Jodie looks at Thomas seriously and shakes her head.

Jodie: "It's not Hannah or Ian now, it's you! You've done what you set out to do.

Hannah's going to be OK"

John has joined Jodie with Thomas.

John: "Thomas, Jodie's right. You've done your share" Thomas: "What's it to do with you?"

John: "I don't want to beat about the bush. That chap with the police, he's a doctor.

He's here to make sure you get to hospital."

Thomas goes to get up but is restrained by Jodie. Thomas (angry): "Over my dead body!"

John: "And that's what it's going to be unless you want to see Lands' end from the inside of a coffin?"

Jodie (angry): "John, that's enough"

John: "No it's not. Up to now he's been ruling the roost. Quite rightly, but, it's about time he learnt the truth! Thomas, you've got an aortic abdominal aneurism."

Thomas: "What in hell's name is that?" The Doctor has joined them.

Doctor: "In layman's terms you have a bubble in one of the tubes from your heart to your stomach. If you don't have an angiography, an operation, now, I can't be responsible whether you will see Lands' End or not!"

Thomas seems to sink back as McLeary, sensing something is wrong, comes and puts his head on Thomas's knee. Thomas looks at everyone surrounding him. Pleading.

Thomas: "Then, it's a good job it's not your responsibility. It's mine"

He turns to Jodie: "Do you not see, lassie, I have to go the whole way. I gave my word and that's my bond. If there's some money left over from Hannah's operation, it can go for someone to care for McLeary? But, what the hell's happening about Ian?"

CHAPTER 12

THE RANSOM

Stephen is reading the front page of The Echo. The phone rings and he pick it up. He listens.

Voice (Strong Glaswegian accent): "You the Editor?" Stephen: "Yes, Stephen McLean"

/voice/: "You want to see the McKeen kid again, It'll cost you." Stephen: "What? Who the hell's this?"

/voice/: "No names, no pack drill. Your paper can afford it. You've been making a fortune out of the McKeen Appeal. Fifty thousand pounds. I'll be in touch."

The phone goes dead. Stephen looks at the phone for a moment and then dials a number.

DISUSED MINE

Josh and Smokey are playing cards and smoking. Ian lies on a sofa, his hands are tied up.

Smokey: "Sheit"

Josh: "That'll be big' Yun?"

He gets up and goes to the phone which is on an upturned cardboard box. He picks the receiver up.

/voice/: "The kid's worth fifty large. Keep him safe" The phone goes dead. Josh turns, smiling, to Smokey. Josh: "the Big' Yun's said fifty large."

Smokey: "He thinks we'll get it?"

Josh: "Hear that kid, you're worth fifty thousand pounds." Ian: "My dad will never pay that!"

Josh: "That's right, kiddo but the newspapers can." Ian: "And if they don't?"

Josh draws the gun from his jeans and points it at Ian's head.

Josh: "We didn't finish your old man off, but, we won't make the same mistake with his kid."

Ian struggles to his feet. He rushes at Josh but is tripped up by Smokey. Smokey: "Your old man should'nae have interfered."

Smokey pushes Ian roughly back onto the sofa.

CORNISH BORDER

One of the policeman comes over to Thomas. He is looking grim.

Pc Trelawney: "That was the boss on the radio. They've put the kid up for ransom.

Fifty thousand."

Thomas: "That makes it all the more important that I don't give up now" John: "Did he say where they were?"

Pc Trelawney: "No, only that the man had a strong Glasgow accent?"
Jodie: "That means they're back in Scotland already?"

Thomas: "I don't think so lassie. It's an old trick. There's no way driving with that jag, they'd not have been spotted." He turns to Trelawney: "They know that everyone will be expecting them to head north and so they'll stay put they're still here in the area. I'd put McLearys' life on it"

John: "I don't see how. Staying where? They wouldn't live rough."
Jodie: "And they wouldn't dare book into a hotel"

Trelawnee: "I'll get on the radio. Have them checking out the local guest houses. You wait here".

LONDON HOSPITAL - DAY

An ambulance draws into the Emergency Entrance of The London Hospital and, as the back doors open, Mary steps out as Hannah, on a stretcher, is wheeled out and through the doors into the hospital.

THE GLASGOW ECHO

As Stephen throws his newspaper in frustration into the wastepaper basket, his phone rings. Quickly, he picks it up.

Stephen McLean. /voice/: "I hope you're busy getting the money together and we hope the police are not getting too busy. That would not be healthy for the kid, if you get my drift, McLean? You've got forty eight hours. We'll be watching the Echo. The headline will read ransom ready to be paid. Then we'll discuss how and when".

The caller rings off, leaving Stephen staring into space.

CORNISH PUB.

Old clay red flooring, old wooden table's pictures in frames on the wall of the Cornish folk and country side. There one old picture of Miner and an old mine.

Thomas and John sit nervously sipping their drinks, their food being allowed to go cold. They anxiously watch Jodie as she puts the phone to Stephen down. McLeary sits just looking at his food in the plate in front of him. Jodie walks back to the table. Around the bar, local people are silent, realizing they are in the midst of an unpleasant drama. Jodie walks back to the table.

Jodie: "Puppets or not, they're pulling they're pulling all the strings. We've got forty- eight hours to get the money"

Thomas: "I've never been a puppet and I'm not going to start now. No clues?" Jodie shakes her head as Policeman # 2 enters the bar and comes over to the table. John: "Any news?"

Policeman # 2: "Afraid not. Nobody resembling our friends anywhere in the neighborhood."

Thomas: "They're obviously hiding out somewhere?"

Policeman # 2: "Aye, you're right but there are too many unused tin mines in the area for us to mount any sort of meaningful search? They've not been in use for years and all in danger of fall-ins"

John: "Any disused military bases? Farm-houses? Ancient monuments?"

Thomas: "All we need is a chopper to scan the area. We may get lucky and see the car parked up."

John: "Expensive operation."

Jodie: "Let me have a word with Stephen. You know how gung ho he is for a scoop." Jodie walks away to the phone.

DISUSED MINE OFFICE.

Josh is trying to get reception on the old television which sits on a table in the corner. Smokey is playing solitaire. He throws the cards on the floor in frustration. As Ian laughs, Smokey gets up and goes to hit the boy. Josh steps between them.

Josh: "Leave it out. The Big Yun does not him roughed up yet. That'll start if they start playing games with us over the ransom. I just want to get this frigging TV going in case there's anything on the news."

Ian: "Let me have a go. I'm always mending ours at home" Josh kicks out at the table as Smoky looks at Ian.

mug"

Josh: "You'r trying Ian? Why would you do that?"

Ian: "I'm as bored as you are and it'll be a change from having to look at his ugly

As Ian points at Smokey who lunges at the boy, but is prevented by Josh.

Josh: "You stupid bastard. Don't you see he's trying to get us at each other's throat?" Smokey grunts and walks out of the room.

CORNISH PUB - DAY.

Jodie returns to the group of men sitting at the table. Their food still untouched but, the look of triumph on Jodie's face gives them hope. She gives them the thumbs up sign.

Jodie: "Stephen says the paper will bear the cost of the chopper for a day."

Pc Trelawney: "That's great news. I'll get on to the powers that be straight away." John: "Have you got a map of the area, maybe we could make a plan of campaign.

What do you think Thomas? This is more in your line than ours. There more way to skin a camel."

Grinning, Pc Trelawney leaves to get a map, Thomas gets up and orders himself another drink.

Landlord: "This'll all be on the house but, don't let it out otherwise, I'll have the whole of Cornwall lining up."

John: "That's very good of you, I'll have a Large Glen."

Jodie: "He'll have a single. I've seen him in action drunk before and it's not a pretty sight."

Everybody laughs as Pc Trelawney returns with a map and spreads it out on the table. Thomas: "That's grand. Now then, we were where when the lad got taken?"

Pc Trelawney points his finger at a spot on the map Pc Trelawney: "And we're here now Pc Trelawney. Thomas gazing at the map. Thinking.

Thomas: "How long before the chopper' get here?"

AERIAL VIEW OVER CORNWALL.

They have an aerial view of Cornwall's beautiful countryside. Finally, the chopper zooms low over the disused tin mine and the black Jag is spotted.

The Pilot talks into the intercom.

Pilot: "Roger. Base. The co-ordinates for the Jag are."

DISUSED MINE OFFICE.

The old black and white television is showing the news. The reception is dreadful. The screen keeps slipping and the sound is distorted. They can just about make out that the search is still on for Ian and the Glasgow Echo is awaiting details of the transfer of the money.

Josh: "There you are, Smoke. I told you, would all work out" Smokey: "How much is the Big' Yun getting for no Risk?"

Josh (sarcastic): "Well, if you remember, you blew a fair chunk of it up your nose and the rest down the sewer. Then there's the hire of the Jag, petrol, food and his cut of the ransom"

Smokey (insistent): "Josh! How much?

Josh: "Twenty... grand is not to be sniffed at"

At Joshes obvious embarrassment Smokey cannot believe his ears.

Smokey: "You mean to tell me that we drive six hundred fecking miles, and are now wanted for kidnapping, for ten grand?"

Josh: "You've put more than that up your nose in a week" Ian watches and listens to the exchanges with interest.

Smokey" "That's nae the point. That was legit business. Sure, there were risks but we knew who and where the enemy was. Now we're on the most wanted list"

Josh: "You've been watching too much TV"

Smokey throws the cards down on the table and storms out of the mine office. As he lights up his fag, he looks up at the noise and sees the helicopter.

CORNISH PUB - DAY.

Pc Trelawney enters and gives Thomas the co-ordinates.

Thomas: "Right! We need to contact the mine owners and get the plans. Do it like an SAS mission"

John goes towards the bar. McLeary barks.

Jodie: "You're right McLeary! I don't think that was part of the SAS strategy and you know it's against the law to drink and drive"

John looks wistfully at the bar but Jodie's words have the necessary effect.

DISUSED MINE OFFICE - DAY.

Ian and Josh are watching the poor reception on the TV when Smokey rushes in and attacks Josh. The scuffle is soon over as Josh bestrides Smokey.

Josh: "What the freck do you think you're doing, man?"

Smokey: "That was a bloody chopper I heard. They'll have seen the car. It's only a matter of time before the police will be here"

Josh: "Stop panicking man. This area is the training ground for the Naval Sea Rescue chopper teams. They're always in the air. In any case, the big' Yun always had an escape route"

Smokey: "What do you mean?"

Josh: "They'll find the birds have flown the coop"

Smokey: "I hope you're right. I'm not ready for another stretch in choky"

CORNWALL ROADS.

Along the narrow roads and lanes of the Cornish countryside, a convoy of cars make their way to the disused mine headed by a police car with Thomas and McLeary being driven by Pc Trelawney, followed by John and Jodie in the Ford.

DISUSED MINE.

Smokey hustles Ian across to the mine lift shaft housing with its wheel stationary They stop whilst Josh looks for the keys amongst a pile of stones.

Josh: "The Big' Yun said the keys were under one of these stones."

Smokey (cont'd): "And then what? You're not thinking of going underground. That thing's not been used for years"

Ian: "I've read about these mines. Many of the shafts have fallen in".

111

Josh finds a key and puts it into the padlock. It's old and dirty on the door. It turns easily and he pushes the door open.

Josh: "Smokey, you going stay here and just let the cops come and get you. I told you The Big' Yun had an escape route"

MINE SHAFT LIFT HUT.

They push Ian forward into the dimness of the dusty Office. Josh goes over to a desk. He picks up a piece of paper from the desk and unfolds it. It is a plan of the mine tunnels. One side of the office is completely taken over by the steel wicker gates of the lift.

Josh (cont'd): "I told you. Now let's get into the lift." Smokey: "I reckon we should leave the kid"

Josh: "you lost your marbles or something? I've not come this far to walk away from the money and, in any case, while we still got him, the fuzz ain't going to touch us. He's our ace in the hole."

As Josh is speaking, they hear the sounds of the convoy of cars screeching to a halt outside. Ian is about to shout out when Josh clamps his hand over his mouth and pushes him toward the open lift door. Between Josh and Smokey, Ian doesn't have the strength to escape.

Bundling him into the lift. They pull the old rusty iron-gate closed. The controls are smothered in dust and large cobweb. Josh brings out a rag to clean it up so they can see the controls wipes and then he pushes the green button. The lift splutters, making a graining sound like metal against metal, as it begins its descent into the dark and glooming mine.

DISUSED MINE.

The convoy of cars have encircled the area. Firstly arrive Thomas McLeary and Pc Trelawney followed by two other police cars. Jodie and John hurry out of the Ford as more police emerge from their vehicles in

Kepler vests, carrying guns and powerful flash-lamps. They spread out around the grounds. Thomas, Pc Trelawney, Jodie and John with McLeary sitting beside them, look around the deserted area.

Thomas: "Hold the cavalry back a while, Trelawney. I want Ian back alive and I started this walk to save his sister from dying not to get her brother killed"

Jodie: "I blame myself. I should never have let Ian come with you"

John: "That's nonsense, Jodie. I'm just as much to blame. I was looking for the big story"

Thomas (curtly): "Lamentations won't help Ian out of this mess"

He takes Ian's bedroll and gives it to McLeary who sniffs it and runs across the ground towards the first mining lift room. The police, Thomas and Trelawney watch and inch their way toward the building. Thomas orders McLeary to stop where he is. McLeary sits obediently, but then stands and runs off to the actual lift hut.

Thomas nods to the assembled crew. He points at McLeary. Thomas /hear a noise/: "That's where we'll find them!"

Pc Trelawney: "That's where the main lift is but the old smugglers always had their own secret passageways within the tunnels where they could operate. There was always one who kept the secret. Passed from father to son. God help the man who betrayed their secrets"

Thomas: "We have McLeary", a boy" McLeary barks

Thomas: "If there's a way out, he'll find it?"

LIFT SHAFT BOTTOM.

The lift comes to a grinding stop in the darkness. As Josh pulls the rusty accordion gates open, so a dim light comes on throwing lights towards two tunnels, each of which have electric lights strung along the roughcast ceilings Josh turns triumphantly to Smokey and Ian. He offers Smokey a large spiffs.

Josh: "Told you the Big'Yun would have it sorted and this'll keep us on track."

Ian: "In these sort of tunnels, you'll not know which is safe and we've got no hard hats."

Smokey: "Then, you'll go first, young'un."

Josh: "There'll be no need for that. I've got the tunnel route maps" Ian: "How long ago were these made? You're both mad!"

Smokey strikes out at Ian and knocks him out. Josh turns angrily on Smokey. Josh: "You feckin'eejit. You going to carry the wee bugger?"

Smokey: "The Big' Yun say how far it was and what happens when get there?"

◆

MINE SHAFT HUT.

Pc Trelawney emerges from the police car having been on the radio and comes up to the group.

Pc Trelawney: "We've managed to track the original owner. A local chap. There are two main tunnels, each having a separate exit point, both of which I've already arranged for men to cover and proceed down"

Jodie: "Then all we have to do is waiting. Are both tunnels safe? We can't put Ian in danger"

Pc Trelawney (nods): "According to him, it was a Scotsman who bought it and he had those two main shafts strengthened and generator lamps installed, but, even if they're cut, there will still be a few working lights"

John is watching Thomas.

John: "Patience is a virtue seldom found in women and never in men, right, Thomas?"

Thomas looks at John with a half-smile and nods. He turns to Pc Trelawney and looks at him enquiringly. In turn, he looks at Thomas.

Pc Trelawney: "Being an ex-Commando man, I think you've already got some ideas, although, risky?"

Jodie (angry): "Will none of you understand? Mary McKeen's just almost lost one child and a husband. What are you thinking of by putting her only son at risk as well?"

Thomas goes over to her and puts his arm around her.

Thomas (softly): "Listen, Lassie. I didn't come this far to let a couple of young skellums ruin everything, let alone put the son I never had the chance to see grow up, in danger"

Jodie looks at him. Tears in her eyes and nods. Jodie: "He who dares wins, right?"

Thomas gives her a cuddle.

Thomas: "Aye lassie. You've got that right."

CHAPTER 13

WHO DARES WINS

MINE SHAFT MAIN TUNNEL.

Smokey is looking anxiously down at the still unconscious Ian when Josh appears carrying a bucket of water which he proceeds to throw over Ian.

Smokey: "What the feck are you din?"

Josh: "I can't wait around all feckin' day for him to wake up. We've got to get moving. The police will be all over Cornwall. Luckily the Big' Yun had two escape routes"

Ian comes drowsily to and struggles to his feet helped not too carefully by the two skellums who are now well high on the spiffs and push him along the tunnel.

Smokey: "And this is the right one, right?" Josh: "Trust me"

Ian: "There's no option is there?" Josh: "You want another belt, kiddo?"

Ian: "you can't afford the time to knock me out again" Josh pulls the gun from his pocket.

Josh: "But with you out of the way. I pull the plug on these timbers which the Big' Yun told me how to do. I tie you to one and get well out of the way. They'd never find you and it would be a tragic accident."

Smokey looks at Josh in amazement.

Smokey: "You're joking' right? What about us?"

Josh: "I told you, we'd be out of the mine and breathing fresh air. Josh smiles and points the gun at Ian"

MINE SHAFT HUT

Pc Trelawney turns to Thomas who stands with McLeary, Jodie and John and a couple of other policemen.

Pc Trelawney: "What do you suggest Thomas?" They are all looking at the lift shaft.

Thomas: "Obviously, the lift's working. Let's get it up and McLeary and I will go down"

Pc Trelawney: "Don't forget they're armed" Pc Trelawney hands Thomas a revolver.

Thomas: "You get your men to those exit points and moving slowly along the shafts.

They've all got the flash lamps, right? Give me one. Thanks!" John: "You want me to come with you?"

Thomas: "No, laddie. You and Jodie get yourselves to the most likely escape route and nab them when they try and escape. You'll have the back up of Trelawney's' men. Come on Trelawney, let's get this lift up. When I get to the bottom, I'll buzz you once for the right- hand shaft and twice for the other one. McLeary will know. You get that generator turned off. Radio your team leaders to warn them and which tunnel to proceed along"

Pc Trelawney goes to the lift operating panel and pushes one of the buttons. There is a whirring sound and the lift wires begin to move.

MINE SHAFT MAIN TUNNEL

Josh and Smokey push Ian ahead of them along the dimly lit tunnel. Josh suddenly stops and holds Ian back.

Smokey: "What's the matter? Josh, you hear anything?"

They stop and listen. They hear the hum of the lift as it descends.

Smokey: "They're coming after us.

Ian is just about to shout out when Josh clamps his mouth and punches him in the stomach"

Josh: "you make a sound and all they'll find is your body. Understand?" Ian nods...coughs.

Smokey: "I dinnae want any part in a murder"

Josh: "It'll be him or us and I already told you about the shaft. Dangerous things, mine shafts. Unpredictable! Stop your whining and catch up, you prick"

LIFT SHAFT BOTTOM.

The lift comes to a halt. Thomas and McLeary step out of the lift.

Thomas shows McLeary Ian's shirt who, having sniffed it goes to the right hand shaft. Thomas buzzes Pc Trelawney once immediately; the light in that part of the tunnel is reduced to a glimmer.

DISUSED MINE LIFE HUT

Pc Trelawney picks up his radio.

Pc Trelawney: "OK West Team. It's your tunnel they're in. Proceed" West Team Leader's voice: "Roger, Commander. On our way"

LIFT SHAFT - MAIN TUNNEL.

The lights suddenly go out on Josh, Smokey and Ian. There is still a flicker of illumination in the mine tunnels but just efficient.

Smokey: "The bastards have cut the lights" Josh: "Nae matter I've got us cover"

Josh brings out a small torch from his jacket pocket. Switches it on.

"This will be enough for us to see where we're going" He shines the torch light down the tunnel"

MINE SHAFT - MAIN TUNNEL.

With McLeary leading the way, he and Thomas slowly edge their way along the main shaft. Occasionally, Thomas has to switch the flash lamp on.

HEAD OF WEST SHAFT TUNNEL

Jodie is standing with West Team Leader at the exit point to West Tunnel. The Team Leader speaks into his Radio.

West Team Leader: "Ok, chaps. It's our call" Jodie: "You're not going without me!"

West Team Leader: "The Commander will have my guts for garters if I let a civilian come with us"

Jodie: "and I'll make sure that the press will have them if I don't go. This my story and I'm going to see it to the end"

West Team Leader is about to call the Commander when Jodie snatches the radio from his hand, throws it as far as she can down the hill, grabs a hard hat and descends into the tunnel. The Team Leader has to follow, gesturing for the rest of the team to follow.

MINE SHAFT - MAIN TUNNEL.

Josh has cut the wire from the now defunct light and with Smokey's help is tying Ian to one of the main support timbers holding the roof up.

Josh: "Looks like the end of the line for you, boyo. If it's that old git' and his dog, you'll be glad to know that you'll all go together. Gag him Smokey"

Smokey takes a greasy rag from his back pocket and proceeds to gag him, but, not too tightly and, with a conspiratorial wink, leaves Ian tied to the support timber"

Smokey: "done and dusted Josh! Now what?"

Josh: "Come on, we'll have to feel our way along the wall to find the switch to trip the roof timbers and then leg it like feck. The Big' Yun said we'd have about five minutes to get to the outside?"

Smokey: "I hope he's fecking right?"

Josh offers Smokey another spiffs. He shakes his head as the two of them begin to inch their way along the wall trying to find the trip switch with their fingertips.

MINE SHAFT - MAIN TUNNEL.

McLeary turns to look at Thomas and begins to wriggle his way along the tunnel toward Ian.

Ian is struggling with his bonds and trying to work. The gag loose, which he eventually does and shouts.

Ian: "Be careful, Mr McLeary. The shafts rigged to collapse at any moment" Thomas's voice: "I've no come this far laddie to let you die for those scum."

MINE SHAFT - MAIN TUNNEL

Jodie, followed by the West Team Leader and his men are using their flash-lights to light their way forward into the mine shaft.

Josh and Smokey, without the aid of flash-lamps, are edging their way along the shaft, fingertips pressed to the shaft walls feeling for the switch which will collapse the tunnel behind them when they hear Ian shout out his warning.

Josh takes a large pull on his spiff and offers it to Smokey who again shakes his head. Josh: "I thought you'd gagged him, you pillock"

Smokey: "I did. You were in such a fecking hurry, he must've been able to slip it."

Josh: "Why do I always have to do everything myself. You're lucky I don't send you back to check him out"

Smokey: "Then you'd collapse the tunnel on me as well and put all the blame on me.

I'm na that daft"

Suddenly, from the other end of the tunnel, they can hear Jodie and west team approaching and catch glimpses of the flash-lamps.

Josh: "Sheit. They're blocking us in" Smokey: "What are we going to do?"

Josh: "If we can find that fecking switch we can still bluff our way out"

Suddenly, his fingers come into contact with one of the trip switches. He turns in triumph to Smokey who is doing a runner towards team west.

Smokey: "I'm coming out. Don't shoot"

At that moment, Josh fires his gun at the retreating Smokey and hits him in the shoulder. He falls to the ground wounded. Jodie is the first to reach him as he crawls around a bend in the shaft.

MINE SHAFT MAIN TUNNEL.

McLeary has reached Ian and is pulling at the wire that binds him to the timber. He helps Ian to set him free and is about to move when they hear the gunshot.

Thomas also hears the shot and shouts to Ian: "Are you alright laddie?" Ian /voice: "Both. Aye and McLeary, we're fine"

Thomas: "OK laddie, we'll have you back in Glasgow in no time". Ian: "Be careful. Remember what I said about the roof collapsing"

MINE SHAFT - MAIN TUNNEL TRIPSWITCH AREA.

Josh stands alone, gun in one hand with the trip switch. With the other he takes a last pull on his Stogie. Clear indecision on his face. He turns to face where has come from and ahead.

Josh (Shouts): "Smokey. Smokey, mate. Are you OK?"

MAIN TUNNEL - WEST TEAM AREA.

Smokey leans with his back against the shaft wall being attended to by a St John man and Jodie west team, Jodie stands in front of him, surrounded by the rest of the Team.

Jodie: "Listen to me Smokey. Tell us who was behind all this. We know about the drugs but we don't know who supplies them. We'll get you protection. I'm sure the police will drop some of the charges against you, especially if Ian and Thomas are safe. The Echo will even buy your story?"

Smokey weighs up the odds and nods: "OK"

One of the west team brings out a miniature tape recorder. Behind her back, Jodie uncrosses her fingers.

MINE SHAFT - MAIN TUNNEL

Thomas, with the aid of the flash-lamp, is making his way gingerly along the tunnel.

Ian stands patiently waiting for Thomas, McLeary at his side. SHAFT - TRIPSWITCH AREA.

As an attempt at bravado, Josh puts his fingers on the trip switch.

Josh (shouting): "Smokey, tell me if you're OK! Otherwise I'll blow the tunnel. It'll be on their consciences if anyone dies.

MINE SHAFT.

Thomas has been looking at the roofing beams. The realization of what he has just heard echoing along the tunnel makes him stop.

Thomas (to himself): "Aye. It's a pickle puckle I'm in right enough but I cannae let them get away with it. Let's see if I can find the trip wires?"

MINE SHAFT - WEST TEAM AREA

Jodie looks at Smokey as he is being patched up. Jodie: "Well Smokey. It's in your hands"

Smokey looks at Jodie and the grim faces around him.

West Team Leader: "The lady's right, my boy. Help us and you help yourself. Your mate couldn't give a flying fig, about you"

MINE SHAFT - IAN's AREA.

Thomas uses his flash-lamp to see if he can find any sign of any additional rigging.

Ian turns and looks down at McLeary, desperate. The dog sniffs the air and suddenly starts digging into the shaft floor. Ian cottons on immediately.

Ian (shouting): "Mr McLeary. The riggings under the floor"

MINE SHAFT - MAIN TUNNEL.

Thomas immediately changes the course of his attention. To the floor. He gets down on his hands and knees and very carefully starts to brush the top surface lair of earth with his hands.

MINE SHAFT - WEST TEAMS AREA.

Everyone is looking at Smokey who has been given a cigarette. Jodie gives him a nod of encouragement.

Smokey (shouting): "Nae problem, Josh. You always were a rotten shot. Missed by a mile. The filth knows we're in charge. They're backing off. As he says this West Team Leader silently nods for his team to back off. Jodie remains with Smokey.

MINE SHAFT - TRIP SWITCH

Josh has managed to dislodge the trip switch mechanism and gun in hand starts to walk cautiously toward the exit.

MINE SHAFT - IAN'S AREA

McLeary's sniffing and scrabbling has unearthed two thick plastic covered cables. Ian looks at them anxiously.

MINE SHAFT - MAIN TUNNEL

Thomas has also discovered the cables. He takes his dirk from his sock and begins to cut into the plastic.

MINE SHAFT - WEST TEAMS'S

There, Smokey, now able to stand, arm in a sling, trying to help.

MINE SHAFT - WEST TEAMS' AREA

Smokey leans against the shaft wall smoking as Josh appears around the bend, gun in one hand, trips-witch mechanism in the other. Josh on seeing Jodie with Smokey immediately stops in his tracks.

Josh (smiling nastily): "Looks like you've found yourself a new pal Smokey? Always thought you were a chicken at heart"

Jodie: "Better free range than cooped up in a cell like one of the unlucky Kentucky variety?"

Josh: "Where'd you spring from Bat-woman?"

Jodie: "Listen! I'm still ready to help you as well as Smokey"

MINE SHAFT - MAIN TUNNEL

Thomas has managed to cut through one of the cables and is busy on the second. Ian is busy cutting through the cables watched by McLeary.

WEST TEAM.

Josh smiles at Jodie and Smokey - he is obviously high. He holds the trip mechanism up to show Jodie.

Josh: "you know what this is Bat-woman?"

Smokey: "It's a trip mechanism to bring the roof down up to the point where Ian is" Josh: "And don't think I won't use it lady?"

Jodie: "Then you'll be done for murder" Josh: "It'll be a tragic accident"

Smokey: "I've told them already. You won't make it Josh"

Enraged, Josh goes to attack Smokey giving Jodie the opportunity to trip Josh up but, in so doing the try mechanism falls to the ground and a red light starts flashing.

MINE SHAFT - THOMAS'S AREA.

Thomas has almost cut through the cable when there is an ominous rumbling sound from overhead and, like a row of dominoes, the timbers come crashing down from behind him. Thomas realizes what has happened and starts running as fast as he can toward Ian's area. Ian hears the rumbling as well and runs towards Thomas. McLeary, sensing the danger runs past Ian when they come to a dead end where the roof timbers have held.

Ian: "Mr. McLeary! Mr. McLeary! Can you hear me? Are you alright"

Thomas's voice: "Aye, laddie. I'm no dead yet but, I cannae move, there's a beam across my legs. Is McLeary alright?"

Ian: "Yes, he's with me now. Hold on, I'll try and reach you"

Ian starts to desperately scrabble his way through the broken, fallen timber. Thomas is lying amidst the debris. Across his legs is a large beam trapping him. His face is screwed up in agony. He is struggling for breath.

Ian, followed by McLeary, is pulling timbers out of the way as fast as he can. Ian: "Mr. McLeary. How are you doing? I can't be that far away from you now?"

Thomas is groaning in pain as he hears Ian's voice very close. He tries to move the beam across his legs but it is too heavy for him.

Thomas: "I can hear you fine and can just about see you through the timbers"

Ian can now also see Thomas and McLeary scrambles through the timbers to his master. Ian follows, being small enough to squeeze through to where Thomas lies. He looks at the stricken man and at the beam across his legs.

Ian: "If I can get some sort of leverage, under that beam, maybe you can pull yourself out?"

McLeary is lying by Thomas. Occasionally, he gives him a lick. Ian hunts around for a piece of wood strong enough to lever the beam up. He finds one and putting it under the beam begins to lever it up.

Ian: "Can you move a little now, Mr. McLeary?"

Thomas tries to inch his way from under the beam. He reaches out toward another timber to help himself pull his way out. Grasping the beam with both hands, he starts to pull away when, with a loud groan, he collapses. Ian drops the lever beam and goes to lie by Thomas who, with difficulty, manages to whisper to Ian whilst ruffling McLeary's hair.

Thomas: "It's nae good, laddie. I did nae tell you but I've got a heart problem. It'll do nae good."

Ian puts his arms around Thomas and hugs him, tears streak down his grimed face. Ian: "You can't leave me or McLeary now, please?"

Thomas suddenly gives an enormous sigh, his face screwed up in pain and falls unconscious in Ian's arms?"

Jodie and the West Team Leader scramble through the debris to find Ian sobbing his heart out across Thomas, as McLeary lets out a loud wail.

ENTRANCE TO THE MINE

A somber group of police, Pc Trelawney, Jodie, Ian and McLeary watch as a team of St John Ambulance carry the body of Thomas on a stretcher away to a waiting ambulance.

John appears with the East Team. He goes up to Jodie and gives her a letter. John: "Thomas asked me to give you this if the inevitable happened."

Jodie accepts the envelope.

Jodie: "Should I read it now do you think?" John: "Maybe you should?"

As Jodie opens the envelope, McLeary comes and sits by her side. She opens the envelope and unfolds the letter within. Jodie take a moment, deep breath, looks at McLeary. He does a small bark.

Thomas's letter's read as follows:

"Dearest Jodie.

I'm not sure quite how to settle this at all.

I have been prepared in my heart that I might not be able to complete this wee trip of mine. Jodie my dear we've crossed many a river and walked many a mile.

But now I must walk alone. It has been my honor to have known you and I am sure that Ian will grow up into a good man, who will always remember the motto of the S.A.S: hand.

WHO DARES WINS

Please Jodie, please take care of McLeary and not too much chocolate. CAPTAIN Thomas McLeary V.C, M.B.E, O.G C, S.A.S DIV 1

Jodie looks over at John and puts her arms around McLeary's neck and holds Ian's

Through her tears, the ambulance disappears out of the mine area.

A minute later a message is conveyed by a policeman to PC Trelawney who turns to

Jodie, John and Ian: "His heart still beats. Maybe there is hope?"

THE END

WRITERS/ NOTE TO READER

Please note that this is not the last we hear of Captain Thomas McLeary's adventures, because he had many more dramatic times before the war with MI6 and after the war as an undercover agent still with the S.A.S and MI5. He had been in many exotic far off place with some names hard to pronounce and had taken on many top secret missions that the British Government could not talk about.

Keep on reading about the Captain and his dog.

SYNOPSIS/TREATMENT

The headline in the in Glasgow Press reads The Hannah McKeen Appeal, followed by – "Hannah's Angel of Mercy is S.A.S hero.

It is the mid 1960's and Hannah, a young girl of eight, lies desperately ill in hospital – she requires donors for both heart and kidneys and the operations, apart from being beyond the financial means of the McKeen family, can only be undertaken by one surgeon, and he is in London. Thomas McLarey and his dog, McLarey, are well known characters in an area of Glasgow where the community spirit is still alive and well and people well remember the bravery and self sacrifice of those who fought in the Second World War. Thomas is now a milkman who serves more than a hundred or so households with milk and dairy produce but modesty keeps his wartime exploits a secret. His dog, McLarey, has been with him since a puppy and is almost human. His grandfather, the original Mclarey served with Thomas during the Second World War and won the canine equivalent of the VC for his bravery along with Thomas's own medals.

One of the first selected to join the elite S.A.S., under the leadership of Jock Lewes, his consuming interest is the history of that Service and he has always tried to live up to it's motto.

Thomas and McLarey are a popular pair in the back-ends and tenements where most of his customers live, particularly with the little gang of children amongst whom Hannah is a member and the children love nothing more than taking McLarey with them to play.

One day, Hannah is missing from the daily milk run that Thomas supplies and he hears that Hannah has been taken to hospital but why, no-one seems to know. He has an appointment the following day with his own GP and discovers the seriousness of Hannah's condition. Meanwhile, the local newspaper has a new editor, Stephen, who is determined to get the paper onto the National news stands. A copy typist, Jodie McFadden, whose ambition is to become a fully fledged journalist and, overcoming the results of an unfortunate first meeting with the new editor, gets the opportunity to accompany an older journalist, John McLone to follow up on that story, as well as one involving Hannah's father, a policeman who has been shot in an attempted robbery. Jodie, by using her initiative, manages to discover the seriousness of Hannah's case and manages to persuade Stephen to get the paper to start an appeal. Thomas, unaware of the Appeal and having just received a copy of the history of the S.A.S. reminding him of his wartime exploits, decides that he must do something to help raise the money for Hannah's operation. He decides to undertake a sponsored walk from Glasgow Central Station to the beach at Lands End with McLarey. After all, Jock Lewes and he walked through the desert of North Africa for thirty days without water during the war, just to prove a point.

Jodie hears of his plan and, despite an attempt at sabotage by McLone, persuades Stephen that this is a story which needs to be told. Stephen sees the potential as a means to getting the newspaper National coverage and agrees to send Jodie, with John as driver and the more experienced journalist, to follow Thomas and McLarey's trip. In the hospital, Doctor Love, under whose care Hannah is, is fighting a losing battle with despite the bureaucracy valiant donations and letters of support on the little girls' behalf. The send off from Glasgow Central is a huge success and is watched with interest by two young hoodlums (Josh and Smokey) who have no scruples about ensuring that the donations reach only their own pockets, in order to pay off a drug related debt to a local gangland chief. As the journey South progresses, so Jodie is able to persuade a reluctant Thomas to relate some of his wartime exploits (the action of which we will see in flashback). This provides added stimulus to the background story which delights Stephen, enhances his belief that his trust in Jodie was well founded and the paper's circulation figures soar. However, the relationship between Jodie and John sours as each day passes.

Not realising that the success of the journey is also being monitored by the ever vigilant Josh and Smokey, one night, the two hoodlums decide that the time is right to strike. However, fortunately for Thomas, John has persuaded Jodie that they should pay Thomas a visit to get more material and between them all the robbery is thwarted. Back in Glasgow, as Hannah fights for her life, there is jubilation. Between the Newspaper, the publicity attracted by Thomas and McLarey and Doctor Love's persistency, the wall of bureaucracy is breached and there has been enough money raised for Hannah to go to London and the surgeon has agreed to operate. Before, Jodie and John can reach Thomas with the good news, he is once more pressed into service when Hanna brother is kidnapped, his life hangs by a thread. Between Thomas and McLarey, they manage to save Ian but, the exertion has been too much for Thomas and his final act of bravery ends in the tragedy of his death.

A story which will exemplify man's goodness to his fellow man and prove the point that:

He Who Dares Wins

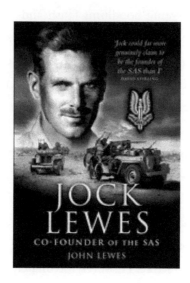

Glasgow Press reads The Hannah McKeen Appeal, followed by – "Hannah's Angel of Mercy is a elite S.A.S hero.

Now a Milk Man who having fought for his country decides to fight against time and the medical bureaucracy NHS(Britten health system)of the Sixties to save a little girls' life. His idea, a Charity Walk with Mr Larey the length of the British Isles in order to raise money for the operation. But a menacing drug gang in the streets of Glasgow, who have kidnapped Hanna's brother and hold him for ransoms. He Who Dares Wins.

Interwoven with daring action sequences from WWII, featuring S.A.S raids into German held territory, is the simple story of a man who having fought for his country decides to fight against time and the medical bureaucracy of the Sixties to save a little girls' life. His idea, a Charity Walk with Mr Larey, his dog the length of the British Isles. A Local newspaper reporter, Jodie her burning ambition is to become a fully-fledged reporter. The new editor, Stephen, is equally ambitious and determined to raise the profile of the paper to that of a national daily Thomas's exploits with the S.A.S, which are re-enacted, add spice and adventure.

Unbeknownst to him, he has been followed on his journey by

Glaswegian thugs who want the money which has been pouring in to his collection bucket to pay off a big drug dealer ambush Thomas, an kidnapping Hanna brother Ian.

Enough money is raised for Hannah to go to London and the surgeon has agreed to operate. Before, Jodie and John can reach Thomas with the good news, he is once more pressed into service when Hanna brother is kidnapped, his life hangs by a thread. Between Thomas and Mr Larey, they manage to save Ian but, the exertion has been too much for Thomas and his final act of bravery ends in the tragedy of his death.

The headline in the in Glasgow Press reads The Hannah McKeen Appeal, followed by – "Hannah's Angel of Mercy is S.A.S hero. Sept 1961

Thomas McLarey and his dog, **McLarey**, are a popular pair in an area of Glasgow where the community spirit is still alive and well. People remember the bravery and self sacrifice of those who fought in the Second World War. **Thomas** was one of the first selected to join the elite S.A.S., under the leadership of the legendary Jock Lewes, whose motto was and still is. **He Who Dares Wins.**

Interwoven with daring action sequences from WWII, featuring SAS raids into German held territory, is the simple story of a man who having fought for his country decides to fight against time and the medical bureaucracy of the Sixties to save a little girls' life. His idea, a Charity Walk with McLarey the length of the British Isles in order to raise money for the operation, captures the imagination of a secretary on the local newspaper, **Jodie.** Her burning ambition is to become a fully fledged reporter. The new editor, **Stephen**, is equally ambitious and determined to raise the profile of the paper to that of a national daily. Despite an unfortunate first meeting, he too sees the potential in the story, especially when Thomas's exploits with the SAS, which are re-enacted, add spice and adventure to the daily reports submitted by **Jodie** However, things do not run smoothly for either **Thomas** or **Jodie.** Assigned to accompany **Jodie** is a seasoned older reporter **John McLone,** who, has already claimed the idea as his own.

He resents **Jodies'** youthful ambition and cynically determines to try and undermine her enthusiasm, and, at the same time get into her bed.

Thomas, too, has his share of problems. Unbeknownst to him, he has been followed on his journey by two Glaswegian thugs who want the money which has been pouring in to his collection bucket to pay off a big drug dealer to whom they owe money. In their haste to get into a position to ambush **Thomas** late one night, they almost run **John** and **Jodie** off the road. **John** and **Jodie** have made an uneasy truce and decide to visit **Thomas** to get some more SAS newsworthy items. As they approach the campsite, they see the car that tried to run them off the road. Immediately, their suspicions are aroused and in an action filled sequence, the two thugs are overcome, **McLarey** has proven his loyalty to **Thomas** and **John** proves to be a bit of a hero as well. Capture the imagination of a large family audience.

A story which will exemplify man's goodness to his fellow man and prove the point that.

:He Who Dares Wins

Thomas Mc Larey and his dog, Mc Larey, are a popular pair in an area of Glasgow where the community spirit is still alive and well. People remember the bravery the sacrifice of those who fought in the Second World War. Thomas was one of the first selected to join the elite S.A.S., under the leadership of the legendary Jock Lewes, whose motto was and still is. He Who Dares Wins.

Interwoven with daring action sequences from WWII, featuring S.A.S raids into German held territory, is the simple story of a man who having fought for his country decides to fight against time and the medical bureaucracy of the Sixties to save a little girls' life. His idea, a Charity Walk with Mc Larey the length of the British Isles in order to raise money for the operation. local newspaper, Jodie. Her burning ambition is to become a fully fledged reporter. The new editor, Stephen, is equally ambitious and determined to raise the profile of the paper to that of a national daily Thomas's exploits with the S.A.S, which are re-enacted, add spice and adventure to the daily reports submitted by Jodie However, seasoned older reporter John McLone, who, has already claimed the idea as his own. He resents Jodie's' youthful ambition and cynically determines to try and undermine her enthusiasm, and, at the same time get into her bed. Thomas, too, has his share of problems. Unbeknownst to him, he has been followed on his journey by two Glaswegian thugs who want the money which has been pouring in to his collection bucket to pay off a big drug dealer, kidnapped Hanna brother. In their haste to get into a position to ambush Thomas late one night, they almost run John and Jodie off the road. John and Jodie have made an uneasy truce and decide to visit Thomas to get some more S.A.S newsworthy items. As they approach the campsite, they see the car that tried to run them off the road. Immediately, their suspicions are aroused and in an action filled sequence, the two thugs are overcome, Mc Larey has proven his loyalty to Thomas and John proves. Capture the imagination of a large family audience. A story which will goodness

:He Who Dares Wins:

A LITTLE ABOUT THE AUTHOR

As a young boy growing up in a white-collar housing estate inventing games to play with my mates, I always had an admiration watching great movies and TV shows, so I found my own adventure by joining the forces. And the rest they say is history.

This book is dedicated specially to my lovely Mum, to all men and women of all armed forces around the world and to my special mates in the hub and everyone that has helped me - friends and mates everywhere.

9 798823 086028